SDP

Sweat Drenched Press

Looking for a Kiss

Richard Cabut

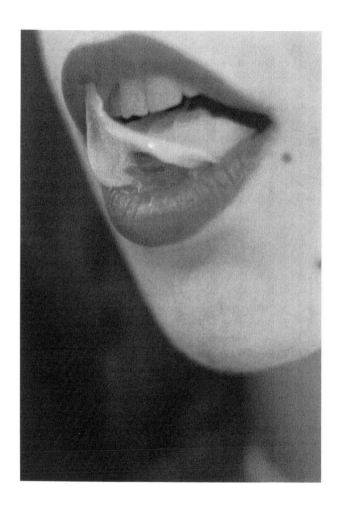

In memory of Peter Cabut, 22nd February 1960-28th June 2020

Recalling the past is always a matter of recapitulating a reality already remembered elsewhere, at other times.
– *Vladimir Nabokov*

 i haven't fucked w/the past but I've fucked plenty w/the future. over the skin of silk are scars from the splinters of stages and walls i've caressed. each bolt of wood, like the log of helen, is my pleasure. i would measure the success of a night by the amount of piss and seed I could exude. – *Patti Smith*, *babelogue*, 1972

A place belongs forever to whoever dreams it hardest, remembers it most obsessively, wrenches it from itself, shapes it, renders it, loves it so radically that he remakes it in his own image. — *Joan Didion*

A true story based on lies, or vice versa. – *Richard Cabut*

Well, listen when I tell ya, you got no time for fix

'Cause I just gotta make it, can't afford to miss

If there's one reason, I'm tellin' you this

I feels bad, bad, bad

And I'm lookin' for a kiss – *David Johansen, New York Dolls*

Comfort for your every need – for every occasion.

1.

blurring the line between observed and sensed experience

Bloop! If colour was a sound, which is how Robert saw it, then that word, bloop! is the sound that this colour or, to be more precise, this mixture of colours would be.

'Bloop!' he said out loud.

It's a stupid word. But Robert was pleased with himself for being able to express it. He was glad, pretty much all over, to be able to vocalise, to describe succinctly, what he saw with his very wide open eyes.

Which was: -

Imagine a child's colouring book to which some annoying kid, anxious to make a big creative impression, had taken the thickest, most vivid wax crayons he could find in the box. But because that kid had been so excited about what he was doing, and because he was only a kid, and a little cack-handed, he had, like most little kids, gone over the black lines. After he had finished the picture, he looked at it and saw what he had done – that he had gone over the lines. *That picture doesn't look proper*, he thought. It didn't look real. So, although he did not really care that much, and felt that, well, in the scheme of things, it didn't really matter – why should you keep within the lines, after all? It's a stupid rule, if, indeed there was such a rule, he would make it better. But he didn't make it better by trying to rub out the bad bits – the streaks and smears of colour – that had gone over the black lines. How can you rub out wax crayon in any case? Even a kid knows that is impossible. No, he tried to make it better by ignoring the black lines completely, by pretending they weren't there at all, and instead filled the whole of the page and not just the parts circumscribed by the black lines, with blazing fuck-off colour. He furiously and feverishly covered every single bit of white, or more like grey, on the colouring page with seething reds and greens and blues. Not to mention amethyst – that's a shade of purple; it was a flash colouring set. Thickly. So, thanks to the texture, the colours seemed to move into each other, as though they were a little alive. Breathing a little maybe. Sliding at the very least. And then that kid sat back and looked at the page with some satisfaction – he had made something new – he had not only gone outside the black lines – he had obliterated them. He now had a page of pure colour that pulsed. This made the boy laugh. He had created, ta-da… art.

And that is exactly what Robert saw. The world in front of him without any solid borders – just a collage of throbbing, primary colours – apart from the amethyst, of course.

And this made Robert laugh. *Well*, he thought, *it is either laugh or panic*. He also thought, *it's a mess. A real mess. But it is my mess*.

The acid that Robert had taken earlier had started to peak.

The drug came in waves – starting with little ripples of unreality – a little smudge to the edges of your vision –

slowly building to big crashing waves of distortion and illusion that could, if you let them, sweep you away in the vicious undertow.

It was a question of sink or swim and Robert had no intention of floundering.

'It's just a drug,' he told Marlene, who had also taken a hit, a bit of blotter. 'It's not real. Just enjoy it – surf it – it's Pop Art! It's Warhol!'

Marlene looked confused.

He added, to clarify: 'It is... Bloop!'

The same sound a big bubble makes when it mysteriously forms and starts to rise to the top of sea. Bloop is the sound it makes as it, well, bloops to the surface.

Bloop is also the sound that the waxy, gleaming, fat colours make as they jostle with each other on the colouring book they cover – like tectonic plates shifting against each other – but instead of creating a grinding noise, they skim to make: bloop.

It is a safe sound. A fun sound. As childlike as the kid's colouring book. As innocent as his attempt to convert the failure into wild success – a picture of his own making rather than one prescribed by the makers of the book.

Safe as Warhol.

Bloop!

The sound reminded Robert that it might just be okay in the end – that , well, he might not be able to distinguish exactly where he and Marlene were – because what was in front of his eyes was a big mess of colours – *my God this acid is strong*! – but that eventually, he would be able to make out the black lines again. The wave had knocked him off his feet – but it was okay, he was secure in big bubble which was protecting him and taking him to the surface once again.

13

'Bloop!' Robert said, and turned away slowly from a troubled Marlene

2.

advertising slogans for the future

Robert peered beyond the colours and was able to make out, not waves like those which had tried to drag him under, but ripples of water. So, that's where they were, by the local canal. In summer darkness, the lighting quality was reminiscent of dusky scenes in some of Peter Greenway's films, especially *Drowning by Numbers* – brim with otherness and the mystical. It was this light which imbued the canal with a sense of romance; enabling it as a conduit of, despite the crap dumped into it, unnatural purity – weaving with the moon reflected on its surface through the margins of something more uncivilised and disorderly. The light and the smell – of shit, piss, blocked drains and something very, very old. The stink took you on a trip and was almost hallucinatory in itself.

He thought, *I wonder if I should mention that this it is all a metaphor*? He thought this because he was a writer and, unfortunately, writers sometimes have those sort of thoughts: everything is like something else, that's the problem.

Or, at least he thought he *might* just be a writer. He wrote about music for the *NME* – although his sights were set on the higher ground, from where you could perhaps see the world and remake it in a way that might be closer to your ever loving/forever hating heart. No one wants to hear about other people's worlds, or dreams – other people's dreams are one of the most boring things, everyone knows that – so the writer, the good writer, is really someone who can manipulate or hoodwink the reader into listening to them talk at length about that strange dream they have just had. So, the writer is a trickster. Robert loved that idea.

If only he had the time, or rather the wherewithal, to write ... soon...

He thought he might just be a writer because in his head he was always describing, analysing, contextualising, recalibrating experiences and feelings within novelised scenarios – in other words, he could sort of tell a story. He imagined another world and other ways of living.

… in between his preoccupations with the hard grip of the night, the ecstasy (not the drug), dreams of tomorrow – always tomorrow – emotional anarchy, physical chaos, and the twin poles, shrines even, of utter freedom and total security and… nowhereness…

Really, though, he knew that writing in your head was not the same as actually writing on paper – putting one, hopefully, beautiful, meaningful, illuminating, not to mention amusing, word in front of the other on paper. Not at all. Even he, in his limited experience, knew that fresh notions, designs and feelings came from the very process of actually writing. The unfolding page itself gave life to new words and worlds. *When language isn't written down it is less than zero,* Robert thought, *maybe there is a God in the typewriter. The Creator. I just tap the keys. I don't know. Who knows? I'm not sure.* He infrequently tapped the keys in a meaningful sense in any case.

… this prevarication would continue into old age. Although prevarication is a weird way of looking at writing: when something is ready to be written, it will be.

Robert also felt like a writer because a psychic once told him that he was. The psychic, in Camden Lock, at the top of a row of shops in the courtyard, looked worriedly at Robert. Psychics are usually expert at softening blows when they think they see bad and sad events coming along. They say things like, 'You will be faced with, um, a very challenging situation. You are lucky! You have the chance to grow as person!' This might be in reference to the vision of some profound personal future shock. But Robert's psychic told him straight: 'You have lost track of the arc of your own life. You don't know who you are. You tell and are told lies. You will be very unhappy. You're a writer aren't you? Yes, yes you are, good. The only thing you can do, the only advice I can give you is: don't ever stop writing.'

Robert thought, *stop writing*? *Maybe I should start*! But, with the unshakeable youthful (Robert was in his early-twenties) belief in all that is wild and messy, that start would be constantly and consistently postponed. A future deferred. Yes indeed, no time like the future.

But looking at the psychic's tarot cards, a Celtic spread pockmarked by Swords – nine and ten for starters – and listening to the way he told the tale, Robert realised that the best writers are like the best psychics: they can tell the future.

He pondered, in simple terms, writers know what is going to happen at the end of the story – or, if that's the way it is, the creative force of which the writer is an agent knows what's going to happen at the end. And, if writing is a ritual – and most, if not all, writers will tell you that it is – then the process of putting one word after another is nothing if not an invocation.

This thought made even more sense to Robert when he recalled it while he was in the midst of his trip. Bloop!

Still ignoring Marlene, he looked at the water for what seemed like an eternity or more, the way it moved this way and that – swaying murkily; both Robert and the canal.

Robert looked at the canal again and saw the waterway as a ribbon stretching not just from place to place but as some sort of amorphous, unlimited, unstructured time stream – past and future – with ambient undercurrents of subliminal meaning – disorienting but always in motion.

Times flies. But it also flows. *This canal*, he resolved, *is all about time, and being able to see what happens as time, the canal, drifts, cascades and sometimes floods – it is all to do with clairvoyance. If I was a professional psychic, I would set up my stall right here. By the canal side. The canal could be used for scrying in the same way as John Dee's crystal ball.*

Robert thought of Derek Jarman's film *Jubilee*, which he had seen several times for the Adam and the Ants footage, and the most truthful depiction of punk of any movie – and never mind Viv Westwood's nonsensical *Letter to Derek Jarman* T-shirt. More recently he'd realised that the film's real significance lay in the John Dee/alchemy/Ariel/time travel scenes and themes. These sparked in him the idea that life was an array of portents and visions for another, future life. Obviously, no need for acid, this lad. It was this occult chemistry that truly *inhabited* the film's viewer, in the same way as the film's first piece of music, Brian Eno's ghostly *Slow Water,* from *Music For Films*, which rendered the rest of the soundtrack almost inaudible on a certain level – in this respect it was magic because it made things disappear. *Jubilee* led Robert to think that even if there is pattern and substance in the universe, this substance is meant to be hallucinatory and arcane. And if it is meant to be chaotic, too, then it also contains a strange acumen which, like the scrying of John Dee, and his like, no one really ever fathoms. *Jarman has surpassed himself*, he thought – plus, Robert really liked Jordan's twinset and pearls.

Robert loved the sense of possibility in writing (and in fortune telling), but worried that he might sound like one of those earnest academics, or even some of the other writers at the *NME* who came across like earnest academics – quoting Nietzsche, or whoever, and noting down their brilliant thoughts in their real Filofaxes. Robert only had a fake one. He also read Nietzsche, or whoever, but wouldn't wear it on his sleeve. Paunches, bad breath, receding hair in their youth, these young men – and they were all men – wanted desperately to be regarded as all-knowing but were afraid to catch sight of their reflections in shop windows for fear of disgusting themselves. Looking in the mirror was out of the question. They trembled with fear, Robert had noted, if ever some young woman, in thrall to their clever words, ever approached them. He hated the way they cited Derrida while making it all sound like advertising slogans – they were the sort of who think there's always a simple answer and who can't understand why we can't just... But, Robert thought, *the world, as they say, belongs to those who can explain it – and these guys seem as though they are doing just that – they are going to win*. They, the fakes and fools, as Robert saw them, are *always* going to win.

Or, perhaps Robert was feeling a little resentful and jealous – he had come to realise that his career was failing, while theirs' was on the up. *No, no, it's not jealousy*, he countered his own thought, *it's like the fight in the 1950s between the Beatniks and their critics*. Those who severely judged their work, their lives.

The Beats were interested in transcendence, the critics only in putting things in dusty boxes. In their tiring search for exactness their lives were half lived. And in their envy, they gave the Beats hell.

Still, a poet can endure anything and everything thrown at him. In response, he or she just writes increasingly miserable poetry.

Robert never wanted to be a 'critic' – that was his big problem at the *NME*.

He thought. *If I wrote this story,* this *very story, about the canal, the acid, Marlene and me, I'd make it, in parts, an unruly stream of babble. But intense. With the liberty to fathom all the forgotten ideas about, maybe, loss of purpose. It would be as much a mood-board as anything, one that would affect the reader as much as something annoyingly posed, depending on the capacity for slo-mo day-glo, or slo-glo day-mo, writing.*

He paused.

*The action would drift like the swirls in the canal –
future and the past. It would definitely need some plot
tension though – something that keeps people reading in
anticipation. Perhaps.*

He peered into those swirls and saw clearly into the
future – the canal, he realised, had rendered him
clairvoyant. He could now tell the future. Just like that.

*Marlene is cheating on me, it's going to get grimy, there
will be pain and deliverance, all at once.*

It's a true story based on lies, he realised. The most
interesting kind of story.

*With the idea that we learn a truth, only to try to escape
from it. But, in escape there's always both pleasure and
pain.*

What a drag. There's always a rub and a kick in the
teeth, too.

He wondered, *is this melodrama enough for people?*

Ah, readers get too hung up on plot anyway, he said to himself.

If nothing happens, everything *becomes meaningful.*

He continued his acid train of thought: *anyway, this story doesn't belong in a book, as such, it needs to be part of an* album. Robert had been reading a book of Verlaine's correspondence, and Stéphane Mallarmé, in an 1885 letter to Mr V, mentioned that the bits and pieces he had written over the years, 'Make up an album, but not a book' – which later sparked the imagination of Roland Barthes, who described the idea of the album – circumstantial, discontinuous, and lacking in structure – as a powerful form of expression because it offered what is usually left out.

Robert liked this idea – he thought it might be revelatory and honest. Or, not, perhaps. He could see, decades in the future, talking about this with a pal, Molly, who said, 'Are we lazy for avoiding structures/procedures or are we right in saying the bits that are left out hold all the meaning? Is it an excuse by the writer who doesn't write? Asking for a friend.'

Robert scratched his head and replied, 'I'm still not sure. In any event, imagined books may not turn out as planned in reality, so let's leave it to the God in the typewriter – not to chance, but to the turn of the page. OK?'

Molly nodded her head and shrugged at the same time.

It might need an introduction, Robert thought about *this* story. *A long one. Sometimes a person's life feels like one long introduction – when is it going to properly start? The truth is, sometimes it never does. The introduction will have to suffice.*

The thought of it made Robert want to run away.

And if I run away, will the words run with me?

3.

bright sad star fell down from the sky

Marlene was jealous of Robert. He was in the safe
world of stupid bloop! She hated him. She hated
everyone. *The cunt*, she thought, *with his fucking
Warhol shit.*

The acid's big bad wave had truly smashed her, and the
undertow had dragged her down into the dreadful
deep. She was trapped there, flailing around in the
depths, miles and miles down, amongst the monsters,
the ugly, blind devils. Dirty devils. Marlene knew they
were down there, she had encountered them before in
that dangerous period just before dropping off to sleep,
tucked up seemingly secure in her and Robert's bed in
her Camden flat. It was in that hypnagogic haze that
there often opened up a little bridge over which
clambered imps from the id.

In the acid deep, meanwhile, Marlene struggled dreadfully along with those mad things. They swam around her, gleefully poking and cruelly cajoling – reminding her of this and pointing out that. The people who had fucked her over, and vice versa. There'd been a lot of both.

Or, the stuff that people called her to her face and behind her back, and said loud enough to be overheard. The stuff that people called out to her.

'That fucking shit Monks single didn't do me any favours,' she told Robert, referring to the 1979 pop punk release. 'Instead of "Show us your tits," ' Marlene remembered, 'the local builders suddenly started shouting out "Nice legs shame about her face." Cunts.'

Never show them it hurts. But it did. The pain, buried and brushed aside, seemingly exorcised via some retaliatory shouts, settled to the bottom of her mind and heart.

Or, the stuff that people said to her while fucking her. One stinking, shitty punk got her into bed, where he looked at her for a few seconds and then, no words, just tapped her flank so she would turn over and onto all fours. 'Nice arse, shame about the face,' he sang, laughing, as he fucked her.

Marlene. Don't cry. And don't come.

And she took every bout of impotence that crossed her bed very personally. Every limp dick was a stab in the ever hating, always loathing heart. She was disgusted by those flaccid pricks – an insult to her face, she imagined, as she worked hard to make them rise while at the same time despising them more and more. Oh, how one guy ran when he saw her bare her sharp little teeth and bend down to his inert crotch. Oh, how Marlene regretted not being quick enough to inflict the necessary pain on him. Soft pricks are *shit shit shit*. She hated hard pricks too, of course.

Or, the stuff that people didn't say to her while fucking her...

Or, her dad. Her dead dad. Whose sad demise some might see as the ultimate rejection and, stretching it a little, as the most severe and permanent form of impotence. The dad who said to her once, 'Marlene, you may not be beautiful,' and then paused before adding, 'but you are beautiful inside.' Marlene knew that he didn't mean it, that he just thought that was something a dad should say to his daughter. They both knew that she wasn't beautiful inside. Or outside, of course. *Ugly ugly ugly*, that's what her dad was thinking, she knew. *Knew*. She fucking hated her dad. He didn't even smoke and got cancer, what a fucking idiot. But she just smiled at him, like a daughter should. Later on, in her teens, he told her she was, 'A mess.'

Marlene. Don't cry.

Or, Branco, who took her to her first punk gig. Johnny Rotten was the only person in the world who Marlene didn't hate. He was God and the Devil and all the saints put together and she knew he wouldn't want to fuck her. He wouldn't care if he couldn't get it up. And neither would she. She wouldn't even bite his cock. Unless he wanted her to.

Branco was her childhood sweetheart. Her favourite person in the whole world, even though she hated him really, along with their friend, Janet, *the fucking bitch*. They were the gleesome threesome, inseparable. Couldn't prize them apart with a crow bar. Everywhere together. They were one – or, one, two, three, four… after they'd got into punk. It was almost a given, understood by all, that Marlene and Branco, *the cunt*, would marry and Janet would be maid of honour, until … no… no …yes!… Branco, tired of the look on Marlene's judgemental and slightly vicious face, left her for Janet. Marlene lost both her *ever fucking loving shithead* boyfriend and her *best fucking cunt mate* in the few seconds it took Branco to reveal his *vile vile vile* betrayal. She never spoke to these pair of cunts ever again.

Branco with his tiny meat. Branco must die. Janet must… Janet with her blue-eyed smile and small tits under her Kings Road tee shirt … I miss her. I really really hate her more than anyone.

Or, Robert, always talking about writing.

Why can't he just get on with it and then he wouldn't have to bore me to death about it. And his mummy issues. His fucking inability to fucking do anything practical – can't change a lightbulb, useless cunt. Not like Colin. Colin can put up shelves. And he's got a van. A blue one. A bit rusty. But useful. Robert can't drive a fucking scooter – one of those kids ones! And his possessiveness – always cramping my fucking style, it makes it hard to get out on my own to… You'd think he loves me. Fucking idiot. And he's always talking about Situationism and Magick. It's all those books he gets from that shop in Camden, Compendium. Boring place. Still, they sell the Anarchist Cookbook – Viv W used images from that on the Vive Le Rock T-shirt. So, I guess it's OK. And his spotty chest – I told him: 'I hate your spots. They look shit.' I could tell he was really hurt. 'Dry your eyes,' I said. 'I was joking.' And I let him fuck me.

Fuck, she hated it. But sometimes he and his cock made her laugh. And sometimes it hurt.

Fuck.

Fuckery. Little known fact, what's a collection of apes called? A shrewdness. So, what is a collection of monsters called? A fuckery that's what. Marlene was being tormented by a fuckery.

'A fucking fuckery,' she mumbled to herself by the canal side.

'What?' said Robert, who had stopped looking into the future for the time being. 'A fucking what?'

'Monsters,' said Marlene.

The fuckery comprised dead people – or, at least echoes or parodies or representations of them. Her dead dad – who, down in the depths, told her again – one more time for bad luck – that she was a *mess mess mess* – that she was messing it all up – messing her life up because she was a mess. Messed up. Just like Sid Vicious' badge. Marlene got the message.

'I'm a mess!' she said.

The dear departed dad didn't hang around for too long. Sometimes when you hang around with monsters you yourself become one. Other times, when you encounter a monster, that monster wonders which of them is the *real* monster.

The foetuses she had aborted over the years were also there, swimming about, as though in their amniotic fluid. They didn't have too much to say for themselves. But it was the way in which Marlene felt that they looked at her which bothered her most. Looks of hatred. Usually, she didn't give a shit what people thought about her after she has done something to them. But after a confrontation with the foetuses, there was only one thing to do: Marlene slumped to the ground and curled herself into, yes, a foetal ball.

She was going to get her revenge though. She was going to be a star. A blazing, falling, bright star.

The world is a heaving bucket full-to-the-brim-of puke and pus with a sparse sprinkling of joy on top – and that sprinkling is made of stardom. They'll all be sorry.

Robert looked into the future again. He saw, decades in the future, Marlene, a ramshackle figure, white face puffed up with booze and bitterness – grotesque and tragic.

'It's the days after the mournings like this that are the worst,' said that Marlene.

For some reason a Gramsci quote had popped into Robert's mind. 'The old world is dying and the new world struggles to be born – now is the time of monsters.' He wondered whether or not to mention it to Marlene. Best not, he decided.

Instead he thought about ugliness and beauty and how things slip through your fingers like powder, and wondered whether or not he had any real sympathy for Marlene, who he knew, would in the future be tiny and exposed and at the mercy of forces that she could never control.

Beauty will save the world, he resolved – what an Idiot.

4.

feelings get bleached out

Back then, 1984, and this will pique the interest of the seekers of untrammeled urbanity and unreconstructed grime, Camden was typically dark, dank, dystopian, and many of the other Ds, too.

It wasn't unknown, in 1984, to come across the sort of mad Paddy that featured in *Withnail and I*: 'I'll murder the pair of yous!' In the Camden backstreets, the boozers were fading testaments to times past, and water passed in the form of piss up against the proverbial wall – and smelling much the same.

But Marlene and Robert were largely oblivious to any of this. They were certainly not poets of the dispossessed. They strutted their Billy-the-Kid sense of cool – bombsite kids clambering out of the ruins – posing their way out of the surrounding dreariness. They were living in their own colourful movie (an earlyish Warhol flick Robert liked to think), which they were sure was incomparably richer, more spontaneous and far more magical than the depressing, collective black-and-white motion-less picture that the 9-5 conformists, or those that stumbled around with their booze-fueled regrets, had to settle for.

They lived in a hard-to-let housing co-op gaff about ten minutes' walk from the tube, on the way to Pentonville Prison or Kings Cross station, depending on which way the chips fell for you.

There was a rehearsal studio around the corner from the house. There, the female receptionist had a thing about *NME* writer Paul Morley. She sent letters to him and he replied in his excitable, frothy prose enthusing about how he would like to take her to the park for some wine and a talk – about his great concepts and theorems regarding modern pop. No one knows for sure if she actually did meet up with Paul, but she soon became dissatisfied with her boyfriend, with whom she stopped having intercourse – but kept giving blow jobs to. Such was the powerful effect of Morley's words – either that, or she was living in her boyfriend's flat and felt obliged to recompense him for bed and board in some way. A *Slaves of New York* situation – Tama Janowitz's hit book, the thesis of which is that finding a cheap pad is so hard in the Big Apple that people in the arts scene stick with bad choice partners just for a place to live. When Robert read the book, he winced. Their flat was in Marlene's name and his position was precarious. He knew, if she became too irritated with him, Marlene would think nothing of asserting her awesome dominance.

She had already started flexing her beefy muscles.

'What did you say to me? You won't fucking say that when you're not living here. When you're out on the street.'

Then in half an hour she would have forgotten that she had ever uttered such a threat – she said all sorts of bad stuff to all sorts of people all the time, if she had to remember every shit thing she said then she wouldn't have any room left in her head for the really important stuff: wanting. She would then, therefore, be completely surprised to find Robert in a bad mood with her.

'What the fuck is wrong with you, misery guts?'

'What you said.'

'What?'

'You don't remember what you said?'

'What? No, I don't remember.'

If he thought it would make any difference, Robert would have said to her, 'I do.' He might have added, quoting Chris Marker, 'Nothing tells memories from ordinary moments. Only afterwards do they claim remembrance, on account of their scars.'

Marlene would have nodded and laughed a little, maybe. She was not yet at the point where she as a matter of course outwardly displayed her disdain. Robert wouldn't have too long to wait for that.

In the future, they would both look back at those scars and have different views on how they had been etched onto their lives. But no matter, truth is often a malleable concept, and there is always a buried truth, a profound truth, behind the apparent, simple one.

Robert grinned at her – but his smile was stationary.

The house was the shoddy shell of a three-storey Victorian building. Other inhabitants included a drama student, his girlfriend and the son of a famous Beatnik writer.

If Robert and Marlene thought that the mad, the bad, the sad were outside in the gaseous pubs and on the claustrophobic Camden streets, then they should have looked a bit closer to home.

One drunken night, the drama student, jealous that his girlfriend was getting on too well with some South American bloke, got up and went out of the living room where the three of them were talking and drinking too much tequila. He went purposefully to the adjoining kitchen. There, on the rusty cooker that had seen its best days in the 1950s, he boiled a kettle. It took a while – he tried not to watch. He did this calmly. Coldly. It was, perhaps, the only known occasion when a kettle was boiled coldly. When it was steaming, whistling at 212 degrees F. When the water was seething in the same way he secretly was, the student dramatically took the kettle, first putting a towel around the handle so he wouldn't scold his delicate actor's hand, and carried it into the living room. There, as his girlfriend sat on the sofa, the stuffing popping out of it, laughing at some joke, he stood above her – *how dare she laugh at someone else's jokes?* – and calmly, coldly poured the scorching water all down her front. The South American remained a witness agog to someone's world in ruin. Her chest, when the doctors were able to cut the clothes from her, was a like congealed lump of bubbling rubber.

Strangely, her hideous screams did not awaken Robert and Marlene, who had retired to bed long before the actor had decided to play this, his most insane role – one that melted his lover to the core. Years later, this actor would appear in a BBC period drama or two. While she, after botched reconstructive surgery, became someone who looked up at you with the eyes of an old stranger if you dared ask if she was all right.

But then it would have taken a lot to wake Robert and Marlene up. They were still young. They were still busy dreaming in Camden Town.

5.

happy recovered

'Happiness is really overrated,' said Robert one day.

He didn't believe in or understand the concept – and thought it was just something that was part of a package designed to get people to leave their family in the morning, struggle through the rush hour, buckle down at some boring work, in order to make money to buy stuff they didn't need which would make them 'happy'.

It was the standard Situationist line/feeling, of course. Robert had read all the books – or at least looked at the slogans and admired the art. But, to be fair, it was something he truly felt, too.

Marlene was on board – after all, the Sex Pistols had been influenced by the Situationists, people said.

Robert would write at length, in a semi-serious fashion, about it one day.

He liked the Situs because they were the guys who best pointed out that people were no longer participants but spectators of life – that what people were living was not real life. With no sense of purpose or any tangible feelings of authenticity, they are separated from themselves and their products. This is because, said the Situs, everywhere and in all areas of human activity reality is consistently replaced by likeness – the society of the spectacle, as they put it. Life has become like a crazy, gigantic advert, they said: 'The economy of daily life is based on a continued exchange of humiliations and aggro; the central function of modern life is to accumulate dead gifts; there is no value, meaning or direction in a world where the logic of the market and the sign conspire to suggest that nowadays, there's nowhere else to go but to the shops.'

With a stylish cockiness, the Situs emphasised that 'work was a disgrace', 'the concept of leisure was an insult' and 'real life was elsewhere – *to be rich today is to possess the greatest number of impoverished objects*.'

Modern society, claimed the Situs, is a closed system, which through the process of recuperation absorbs and negates opposition and critiques. It is a feedback system akin to the type of artificial intelligence systems that information theorists dream of. And against this unreal avalanche of things real – Situationist practice was a glorious, 'Non!' to the world of television, consumerism, alienated work, holidays in the sun and 'happiness'.

So, Robert sometimes liked being sad. In fact, it was his duty.

In the early days of the relationship with Marlene, there was nothing much to be sad about. The pair were, to all and intents and purposes, happy. This wouldn't do.

Robert initiated what he called regular sadness sessions. On an evening when nothing much was happening, they would lie on the bed, turn out the lights, close their eyes and listen to melancholic music from Robert's collection – Marlene only had a handful of records (*Never Mind The Bollocks*, *Bill Haley and the Comets*, etc) – Joy Division, Leonard Cohen, Puccini, Mozart, Lou Reed, Nico, Otis Redding. The usual. Anything in D Minor – the saddest of all keys, if *Spinal Tap* was to be believed. They would listen and reflect.

Robert thought about: his late sister Daniela, an artist and designer, killed in a car crash in '73; his mother – of course he thought about his mother – who had been driven insane by the death of her daughter (and death lived in Robert ever since then, too); and the very fat woman he had seen that day in the nearby alley who was trying to carry her shopping home and struggling so hard just to put one foot in front of the other – shoes on the point of splitting away from her bulging feet. Almost dropping her food but not giving up and the sweat pouring down her face and into the fold of her neck, and her fixed grimace of determination in the face of all of it, every single bit of it – *this life*. Her road must have seemed endless.

It all made Robert want to cry – but it also made him feel good. The sadness hooked him into the world, and into the meaningful events in his own life. The sadness

46

was a black hole he could plunge into that would result in radiance of sorts. He wanted to cry about the ghost of his sister, his mother and the beautiful struggle of the fat woman – and then he wanted to wipe away all the tears, including his own. He hated soppy moralising. He liked being haunted. *Well, it's better than TV*, he thought.

The sorrowful energy was almost touchable. Like, if not velvet, then the cheaper version: velour. Like Marlene felt between her legs.

He always felt like sex afterwards. And he always felt like writing, too. Maybe at the same time. Why not?

I write best when I cry. I write best when I cry and fuck.

He reached out in the darkness, in his head, for a connection to Marlene. But: nothing. He just felt like all the other lonely people who are convinced that their self can find no essential link – or even understanding – with another self.

What a monumental melodrama, he thought. *A right old palaver.*

Anyway, he thought, *it's not about understanding, it's about feeling.*

He felt like he was understanding something about detachment, by sensing, senselessly, the murk outside the window, and the bitter cold in the Camden streets, the dog shit by the kerb, the human shit by the canal side. He caressed this thought of the wilderness and knew that in the expanding gloom every form of dread could be expected.

It's all a car crash, he felt.

Marlene joined in the sadness sessions because she hadn't yet started saying 'no' to each and every one of Robert's suggestions about anything. She hated the idea of feeling sad. It was stupid. She hated the idea of closing her eyes. If she closed her eyes too often, there was always the danger that the voices would start their *fucking shit.*

*Dead dad. Some dead kids. Who needs them? Fucking
idiots. Leave me alone.*

Alone in her head and unconnected. Isolation. *Just like
that stupid Joy Division song. Ian Curtis, what had he
ever had to moan about? Cunt was a star.* 'Mother I tried
please believe me' – *I fuckling hope Robert is listening to
this – this is where your mummy's going to get you – a
rope around your neck.* 'I'm ashamed of the things I've
been put through. I'm ashamed of the person I am' –
*that's where you went wrong, Ian, me old chum – no
shame, that's my motto. No fucking shame.*

Marlene was shameless. Instead she thought of exactly
how she would kill that *fucking cunt Branco. Let's be
friends? Let's be foes. Even better, let's be strangers.
Tears are not enough – there will be pools of blood. Kill.*

Her thoughts were in monochrome – giving her the
feeling and pressure of a migraine in black and white.
An austere psychological aesthetic. It all droned on in
her head nihilistically.

Robert and Marlene, the happy couple.

In fact, Marlene would have given anything to be happy – she hated happy people because she was envious, and she wanted to slaughter their happiness. Nothing made her happier than breaking up a good friendship. *That will fucking teach them*. She hated the looks on the faces of happy people – that disgusting openness that said yes to everything, all the 'connectedness', all the 'inquisitiveness' about everything even all the bad shit, like… *everything*.

It gave her a headache. Thinking about it. In the dark, listening to *fucking Joy Division* she focussed her mind on the actual neurons and synapses in her head. And was puzzled. Something was wrong.

Maybe the fucking speed has torn holes in my head, she worried.

Or, in her soul. Her arsehole.

It made no sense, she thought, brokenly: *defined in negatives; what I hated hated hated what depressed me, despised, gave voice to gut deep disgust it was a pose but ugly. I am afraid. I am making no sense.*

Something *was* wrong.

They expected me to just swap roles. I would become the best friend. And she would be the girlfriend. Janet. Best friends. Fuck off. My best friend was speed. Like Johnny said: It's all I need. All.

After the big split, Marlene snorted and snorted and snorted amphetamine sulphate until it burned out her feelings – and until she herself burnt out, in roughly the same way as Jimmy in *Quadrophenia*, smashing her scooter (she briefly toyed with Mod) and going bonkers. She quickly became one of those dangerous people playing with fire that other people tended to avoid; like they would skirt around an angry looking, mad dog. Some new boyfriend found her one day sitting in cupboard, talking about voices.

It is all a crash, she felt.

On the bed, in the dark as Joy Division finished, Marlene opened her eyes and blinked. Robert stirred beside her.

I don't want to be screwed, thought Marlene, *and I don't want to feel anything.*

Robert thought: *I want to be screwed, and I want to feel something.*

6.

one of the charms of desire

Curled up unsafe and unsound on the canal side, Marlene realised she had to move. She didn't care about people seeing her in this state, listening to voices in her head saying bad stuff to her. She had even stopped whimpering a little. But her bladder was bothering her.

'How are you feeling?' Robert asked, fairly cheerily.

'They're talking to me,' she said. 'I wish they'd fucking stop. Well, the dead babies aren't talking. They're just giving me shit looks. It's my dead dad, I wish he'd fucking shut the fuck up.'

Robert shook his head: voices of aborted babies – that sounds like some stupid and bad advert for a Pro-Life group.

In his head, Robert was writing this story, the one he and Marlene were enacting at that very moment by the canal. And he was also worried about the appearance of the dead dad. There are too many of them in literature, Jesus in Gethsemane, Superman and Jorel, not to mention tons of Greek Mythology. It can be indicative of lazy writing. This perturbed him. Yes, of course he was lazy, he'd much rather be living in his epic dreams with a reckless gait than sitting at his desk and writing properly – it was hard enough just getting down to his music writing for the *NME* and *ZigZag* – no wonder he wasn't getting anywhere. But he wouldn't like to be thought of as a writer who was cliched. Perhaps, in the story, he'd have to change the father to the uncle, or something. *No, too* Hamlet. *Not that there is anything wrong with a bit of Hamlet. Anyway, it makes sense to establish a main character's relationship to their parents.* He decided to leave the dead dad in, for the time being.

'Are you having a crisis?' Robert asked, even though he knew she was. 'Don't worry, it's common for people to draw on the spirits of their deceased when...'

Marlene stopped listening to him. Yes, this acid trip was a crisis. But it wasn't just about this – her whole fucking life was a fucking crisis.

'I've got to move,' she mumbled.

'Just take it easy,' Robert advised.

'I need to go for a piss!' she exclaimed.

'Bloop!' said Robert.

'Not a poop, a piss!' said Marlene a little more forcefully.

Her bladder was approaching bursting point – before taking the acid they'd had a few pints in the Prince Albert, on Royal College Street, near the canal. This boozer served as a local for their friends who were part of the hippy and punk arts and farts community centred in nearby Georgiana Street.

The acid had now peaked. It would remain strong for another few hours. But the crux had been reached and passed.

It's downhill all the way, Marlene thought to herself.

Robert, too, could now make out ever more strongly the black lines of the colouring book. At least he could say other things in addition to bloop!, which he continued to utter now and again, to keep his hand in – and because he knew it was driving Marlene mad.

'A piss?' he puzzled.

Marlene didn't bother answering. She had three choices. One: go back to the flat. But that was ten minutes up the road, and she probably wouldn't make it. Two: go back to the pub, but she could not face anyone at that moment. Three: go for a piss by the side of the canal.

Ordinarily, she would have had little problem in simply pulling down her pants and having a coy squat with her arse stuck out a little, before letting go.

Having said that, she was not a toilet extrovert. She was not a nonchalant or lavish user of the lav. Some couples don't care. They will go to the toilet without closing the door – and piss and shit while talking to their boy/girlfriend. And not just shit carefully, controlling the sphincter so that the turd slides out making little sound apart from a small splash when it hits the water. No, some people will fart copiously, the sound echoing around the bowl, loud enough to drown out the radio or stereo playing in the next room, perhaps. All the while talking normally or joking to their partner, as though nothing unusual was going on. Which, of course, it wasn't.

That was not for Marlene. When she went to the toilet, she made sure that the door was closed. If Robert or anyone else was in the small flat, she made sure that some music was playing to mask any sound she might make. She particularly liked those toilets, public, or in other people's flats, with a fan that started up when the light was switched on – not just because the fan would extract the smell but because the noise it made would allow her to shit without fear – the fear of being heard shitting, there must be a word for that.

Marlene didn't care what people thought of her, it is not that she wanted to maintain some kind of demure, prim, her-crap-don't-smell mystique. Neither was she worried about destroying any sense of romance with Robert with a familiarity that breeds contempt (farting competitions in bed and other such scatological nonsense). She had enough contempt to go around without the need for familiarity. With Marlene, toilet reticence was simply the result of... some Freudian shit.

But this was an emergency. She wanted to piss. She wanted to piss badly... if only... it suddenly came to her, in a flash (in the pan), if only she could piss on *all the fucking fuckers who had fucked with me. Who had shat on me. Yes, piss on them all!*

She dragged herself up from the floor with a sense of urgency and enthusiasm – now pissing was not a simple evacuation of the bladder, it was revenge.

She stayed in the middle of the canal path, not even moving to the grassy side – too much dogshit. God how she hated dogs. Her hatred wasn't reserved for humans. Snarling bastards. Drooling. With their teeth. Fucking teeth. Smearing their shit everywhere – getting it on her Vivienne Westwood boots – or, for a fraction of the price, replicas made by a Greek cobbler in Camden whose shop was not far from this exact spot – just as good as the originals because he was the guy who made all of Viv's boots anyway. *And if I had a kid*, she thought to herself righteously, well, *that kid could be, would definitely be, blinded by dogshit.* Marlene would never have a child.

She did not care if she was seen, she did not want to hide – this was retribution, and that had to be seen to be enacted in order for it to be effective. To act as an example to other potential transgressors.

There was no need to pull her trousers down. The zip of her bondage trousers stretched all the way around the crotch to the buttocks. She wasn't wearing knickers – not for any other reason than they had not bothered to do any laundry for ages. She squatted and opened her legs.

Robert looked on, with some amusement. Bloop!

Marlene, contorted her face, putting her tongue between her teeth, something she always did when concentrating, and pissed.

She closed her eyes.

She let the beery water run out of her body, and heard it hit the concrete.

Robert wondered: *is there anything more urban than the smell of piss on concrete?*

Marlene had once heard someone say that she – *me!* – was as shallow as piss on concrete.

She imagined, she saw, she tried to manifest, the person who said that underneath her arse. That person, Marlene pictured, was part of a crowd that included Branco, her dad, all the mockers, her mum – *no, not my mum! – Janet, all the wankers who had fucked me*, who had stolen stardom from her, who had ignored her. And Robert? Of course, Robert! All of them, jostling under her arse, with their mouths open, kneeling underneath her as she dispensed, from a height, urine justice. They drank. Gagged and drank what she gave them. Doctors, former employers, people who had not given her the proper kudos, who had not paid her quite enough homage. She laughed: *the future is an open gaping mouth drinking and gagging on my piss.* An endless stream from a bottomless bladder.

Branco, Janet, Robert, anyone, everyone – *not Johnny Rotten!* – gasping! Gagging! Wretched and retching. Humanity doused in her waste.

Laughing loud now, she muttered – 'Baulking at my piss, whatever will you do when I shit!'

Did I say that out loud? She wondered to herself, although she didn't really care one way or another.

'What?' Robert came out of his trance. He had been staring at Marlene pissing. He admired the functional

61

nature of the zip on the bondage trousers. How clever. Designed for quick access during sex in the bog, or wherever, of course. *All trousers should have such zips*, he mused. And, *she should have worn her Seditionaries' Marilyn Piss T-shirt*, of course she should.

But mainly he admired the piss-off attitude Marlene exuded while pissing, the way she squatted, her legs apart – shameless rather than the sham that usually characterised the approach to her own body – to sex. To having her legs apart in any fashion.

This amazed him.

But what amazed him more was the piss itself as it cascaded down onto the path. Not the fact that it looked like a waterfall. Crashing down. Powerful. Awesome – he looked at it in the same way that people looked upon the Niagara Falls, maybe. But its colour – why, the stream was not boring yellow, but red, and green, and orange, and violet and blue. He was impressed.

Everyone can sing a rainbow. But Marlene can piss one! Bravo.

The froth, though, the foam it created when it hit the ground – that was pure white. Quite a trick.

Then Robert saw something else.

'Look!' he pointed at Marlene's urine.

She opened her eyes and was a little surprised to see Robert standing in front of her rather than underneath, gargling her urine.

'Look,' he repeated, pointing.

She looked down, saw the puddle between her legs. *What was he referring to? The amount of yellow piss?*

She followed with her eye the stream of urine as it flowed to the side of the canal and then down, into the water itself.

Ah yes. That's what Robert was on about – *how one thing flows into another. Everything. How things merge. Even piss.* Especially piss.

Ha. Pathetic and ever so slightly profound all at once with a touch of irony thrown in for good luck. A bit too fucking Zen for everyone's good. That is what she loved about Robert sometimes – *no, no, no, no not love.*

'Every little bit helps,' Robert said, as they both watched the piss flow into the canal.

She nodded.

Marlene finished pissing. She felt satisfied. She felt better. Wrongdoers had been disciplined. *Drink piss, muthafuckers.*

'Kiss this,' she said, slapping her own arse.

This was one of the things that made Marlene seem ludicrous, Robert felt – her penchant for quoting Sex Pistols lyrics at every and any opportunity. Finding or underlining significance in the everyday through references to pop songs, or vice versa.

If a friend was going on vacation – Marlene: 'A cheap holiday in other people's misery!'
If someone looked at her blue hair – Marlene: 'Well they're staring all night and they're staring all day.'

And so on.

God, it was tedious.

How about 'You're a liar?' thought Robert.

As for 'I'm not an animal' – *let's not go there.*

In the distance, they heard a bunch of people coming their way. Shouts, grunts and drunken bellows in the night.

Robert smiled: in the story, now would be the perfect opportunity to introduce a chase scene. Establish some of that much needed tension: Marlene running fast, while trying to zip up her trousers, Robert running even faster. Knives flashing In the dark. The thud of angry boots. 'We're going to cut you from ear to ear, from here to here, fucking punks. We're going to slice your guts open and chuck your fucking innards around for fun. We're going to jump on your spiky heads and throw you into the canal.' Then Marlene falls, Robert looking back, has a choice... try to save Marlene, or make good his own escape. Tension within tension. Ooh.

But, no. Too crass. Robert couldn't be bothered. And he knew that if there was such a choice to me made, he would try to help her. He also knew that, if roles were reversed, she would *fucking well not.*

'Let's go home,' he said to Marlene.

They staggered to the steps which lead up to the road.

Marlene turned and shouted into the night.

'You're as shallow as piss on concrete!'

Silence.

7.

under the thrall of forgetting

Walking up the street to their flat, Robert, despite moving away from the clairvoyant canal, could still see the story, their future, unfold.

A little while in this future, he could see both of them on the bus up Haverstock Hill to the Hampstead Classic where they watched *Withnail and I*.

This film had a big impact both Robert and Marlene.

The journey back was made in silence, the atmosphere one of suspicion. They gave each other the odd penetrative look – jealousy.

Both of them identified with Withnail – the unreconstructed, hopeless, boozer and loser.

Marlene was something of a professional punk, while at the same time working shit jobs for speed and booze money. The housing co-op rent was nothing. Food? *Fuck all.* They lived on lentils. However, Marlene had got the wrong idea about punk from the very start. Punk was, in effect, a way of stopping your past from becoming your future. But from 1976 onwards Marlene was trapped in that punk moment – like a fly in piss coloured amber. No wriggle room forever. Punk had not freed her, she was instead imprisoned by the character she had assumed at that time. Just like her hero Johnny Rotten, who seemed to have, or portray, only one emotion over the course of his whole career and life: anger. Bad energy forever. Marlene's life was underpinned not by momentum but by nostalgia.

Robert could see in the distant future, at retirement age, Marlene – on prescription pills, ravaged by lassitude, mental illness, incuriosity and defeat. In an age characterised by identitarian politics, and the virtue signalling therein, her solidified identity remained: virtuous and angry punk.

Marlene *fucking hated Robert* – in the film he was I, and was going to escape the squalor and waste and embark on a career. *He was going to fucking fulfil himself. She* was meant to be the *fucking star*! *Stardom stardom stardom*. She craved it, she could see it, she could almost taste it.

'The film tonight,' Marlene came out with it. 'You are I and I am Withnail!'

'I am I?'

'I and I?' Marlene misheard, wondering for second why Robert was using the Rasta phrase?

'What? No... I am not I! I am Withnail,' he insisted. 'You are I!'

A compromised was reached.

'We are I!' Robert said. 'You and I are I!'

'You mean, we are Withnail!' Marlene corrected.

Withnail and we.

Robert also saw himself at a point in a nearer future, only a few years away, sitting at a desk and writing in a diary: 'Am I a man or a slug slithering into oblivious obscurity leaving a shiny/dull trail that people, if they notice it, probably won't even wonder what happened to the slug that made it.'

Fuck, thought Robert. That's a bit melodramatic, mate. Tone it down.

Ultimately, Robert didn't think of himself as a loser. In a way he was arrogant and entitled. People like him weren't losers – of course they weren't! They were, he liked to think, mavericks, free spirits, bohemians, nonconformists. Their lives were utterly extraordinary and enormous and dizzy. They were never poor or penniless. They could be standing in the road begging, it didn't matter – they were completely superior to such mundanity – having zero makes it even easier to be foolish and facetious.

All that mattered to him was maintaining a solid sense of *sprezzatura*, an all-consuming cool.

Robert and Marlene, were eternal youngsters keen to live in a film, overwhelmed by the idea, but knowing that in one way it wasn't real and would have to finish. The End. Credits.

At the start, Robert and Marlene were in lust with autonomy, abandon and deliverance.

They vibrated with youth – an economic design, not particularly calculable in age. They were amongst those who were through, for instance, apathy, disgust, drunkenness and disaffection omitted from the fiscal life of society, and who sometimes saw themselves as auguries of freedom from tradition, family, labour. Youth has nothing to lose but its sense of adventure.

They played like kids – not for nothing was one of Robert's favourite books the hippie ideal for living *Playpower* – but felt like transformative agents, communicating to others the dangerous stultifying nature of everyday life.

They were in tune with their universe. There was no
end to their thirst and hunger for desire. Their passion
for the world – for *their* world – was limitless. Robert
and Marlene thought they could see what real life could
be offer; euphoria and elation. They lived on and for
craving. Youth is all about wanting. Wanting what?
What have you got?

They proceeded to attempt to achieve their dream of
complete and permanent personal, cultural and
spiritual intoxication and glory by... *wasting time.* They
only picked at their art.

They also picked each other's spots sometimes. The
ones on their backs where the other could not reach.
Black heads, white heads, red heads – so intense were
these sessions they seemed to enjoy it more than giving
(which was a given as far as Marlene was concerned)
and getting head. Certainly, the spot picking sessions
sometimes lasted for hours, much longer than their sex
sessions – and were definitely more intense. They
would go over each other's clogged pores, searching for
imperfections and eruptions. That Robert and Marlene

72

marked/celebrated their coupledom in the context of purulence said something about their relationship – that it was pockmarked by the wrong sort of dirty. But picking their spots may have been preferable to picking on each other.

Robert and Marlene, the daydreamer and the idler, agitators and objectors to the world of the regular and the routine. They lived in some sort of self-exile, in an ivory tower. The mistake they made was building it on sand.

They thought they would be forever young, so to them time was of little consequence – however, it was the world which grew older around them.

Peter Pan said to me: growing up, baby, means giving up your dreams.

Being an old has-been punk is a morbid thing, but being an atrophied never-was punk was worse.

And some would say that calling a life unorthodox is just a way of avoiding giving a harsher name to your defeats.

Robert and Marlene, after a while, became fearful about a non-existent future. They were both free, with free time – but, they wondered, *free for what*? And, brutally, they were often reminded that books, music, booze, drugs, holidays (they only made it as far as a caravan park in Hastings, but still…), trips (both varieties), don't come for free.

The couple had managed to suspend and set aside the impact of the unfolding years, the thought of which left them shaken and petrified.

Marlene demanded stardom.

Robert demanded recognition.

Both: for what, remained a constant mystery. Especially to themselves.

Outside, they recognised that the world had somehow, while they were dreaming of poetry and chaos, assumed its form of consumer and market culture – people, former friends, everyone except them seemingly, were getting on with their careers, signing record deals, book deals, becoming journalists on the nationals, advertising executives, fashion designers, models, furniture makers, jewellers. They were buying suits, flats, better drugs, travelling to New York regularly. Everyone was splashing around in the soothing bath of luxurious passivity and progress. People were following the cash and the party bash. It was the 80s after all.

Robert and Marlene were still playing. But in that context their play was no longer fun.

Failure became their default setting – and they made the mistake of glorying in their assumed roles of hapless also-rans – you could hear the exultation in their voices as they itemised hardship and calamity.

The couple were drinking a lot. Robert especially found that his centre would and could not be deluged with the creation of sentences, paragraphs, chapters and then books, so instead he drowned it with lager and disgust.

Attempts at creativity barely acted as reminders to the universe of their presence, but acted, nevertheless, as sincere prayers for succour and safety from a future they were unable to activate.

But usually, they were left unfulfilled, unsatisfied and sure that these prayers would remain unanswered.

In their hearts and souls they realised the truth: the blind universe doesn't give a fucking shit, and nothing, absolutely nothing, exists until you yourself make it.

But they did not know how to make much apart from peril and pitfall for themselves. They suffered from paralysis. They could not reinvent themselves or fight back against a dangerous foe because the foe was, of course, themselves.

Their tightly sealed world – an airless chamber – in which, yes, all their ideas were the stuff of genius, and all their conversations were revelatory, and all their jokes were the most amusing anyone had ever heard – but only because no one else ever heard them – their gags were uttered and made sense only to themselves. And in the end not even they laughed at their own jokes.

Amongst it all, the growing sense of exhaustion and desolation, Robert thought they would be saved because they were in it together for ever – they would keep each other warm in a cold world from which they had been frozen out. The Fool.

But everything they had – shared beliefs and emotions – rested on and consisted of thin, rank, stale air. Theirs was not a life, but a retreat. Punk had glamorised concepts such as chaos and blankness. But when Robert and Marlene started living out the words that had previously been written in biro or felt tip on their T-shirts, they found it almost unbearable.

No future.

We are not in the least afraid of the ruins.

In fact, the ruins petrified them.

Robert, walking with Marlene to their Camden flat, knew that it would not be easy for the hapless couple to navigate themselves out from the debris of their own deflated dreams, to free themselves from their own story.

He looked at it coldly, and objectively. The unfolding story. That was the important thing. Ultimately it was the question of what lay under the surface, unknowable, that was so beguiling, raising questions which should be routine like, why oh why must the world consist of a tearing and grinding that approximates the rage and sadness of breakdown, and faded emotions?

Robert said to Marlene. 'I have of late, but wherefore I know not, lost all my mirth and indeed it goes so heavily with my disposition that this goodly frame the earth seems to me a sterile promontory; this most excellent canopy the air, look you, this mighty o'rehanging firmament, this majestical roof fretted with golden fire; why, it appeareth nothing to me but a foul and pestilent congregation of vapours.'

He paused.

And added: 'What a piece of work is a man, how noble in reason, how infinite in faculties, how like an angel in apprehension, how like a God! The beauty of the world, paragon of animals; and yet to me, what is this quintessence of dusk. Man delights not me, no, nor women neither, nor women neither.'

She said to Robert: 'Oh, shut up, for fucks sakes. Just for once, shut the fuck up. Fucking idiot.'

She didn't want to *fucking hear it.*

Say 'Yes'. Feel like a million. Why accept less?

8.

frozen at centre of the frame during passage of time

One day in the future, or in the past, depending on where you're standing. Marlene and Robert were graced by the visit of Eddie, Marlene's nephew. They had agreed to look after him for the day while Marlene's sister sorted out her divorce.

'I hate that kid,' Marlene said.

'Yeah, I know,' said Robert.

That kid and every kid. But this kid would do for now.

Eddie was autistic, so when they took him out to West End they had to be quite careful. Eddie would just wander off, drifting happily, oblivious to any potential danger that the Metropolis might have in store. While Marlene and Robert browsed in the larger shops, it was easy to lose sight of him for a few minutes. Then the hunt for Eddie would begin.

'Ah, fuck him,' was Marlene's attitude. 'He'll turn up. Look, what do you think of this jumper – it's real shit isn't it. Not exactly Viv Westwood is it? Fucking crap.'

But Robert felt sorry for the kid. He had enough shit to contend with, and was sure to have a lot more soon. Robert went off to look for him. But after fruitlessly searching all the aisles in all the various departments, he began to worry. Robert went back to where he'd left Marlene, but she was no longer there. Concerned, he looked outside and was relieved to spot Marlene with Eddie, down the road. They were looking at something on the wall. Staring at it intently. Robert wondered what it could be, and getting a little closer, saw it was a daddy long legs. In fact, it was the daddy of daddy long legs with the longest legs of any daddy long legs Robert had seen. Amazing in a way.

Eddie was enthralled, unable to take his wide eyes off the remarkable insect.

'Do you like it?' Robert heard Marlene ask.

Eddie did not answer. He merely stared.

Marlene looked at the insect, then at Eddie.

'Do you want to kill it?' Robert heard her ask.

Eddie said nothing.

Marlene took his hand in hers, and straightened out his thumb. She put his hand up to the wall, to the daddy long legs.

'Are you sure you want to kill it?' said Marlene.

Eddie said nothing, just kept staring.

Marlene smiled, thin lipped, and putting Eddie's thumb on the insect squashed it hard, smearing it down the wall until all that remained was a few of those long legs stuck to the wall. Gone daddy gone.

Robert was shocked.
Eddie looked vacant.

'Don't run away again, okay?' said Marlene to the boy.

'What's going on?' asked Robert, approaching the pair.

'Nothing,' said Marlene. 'I was just telling Eddie not to run away anymore. Anyway … so… that shit jumper, I ripped it a little, and put back on the shelf, made it a little more punk. Ha ha. Let's go down the Kings Road, it'll be shit but everywhere is shit now, but fuck it, what about you Eddie? Eddie wants to go down the Kings Road, yeah? Auntie Marlene had some good punk times down there. And after popping into Viv's we can go and laugh at the Boy clothes. Then maybe pop into the Chelsea Potter, have a pint and get some speed. Oops, don't tell your mum I said that will you. Ha ha. And then we can see who's around and see …'

Marlene talked on as they walked.

People who talk too much, incessantly, sometimes do so because they are needy and empty, and wish to fill that void with words. Any words. But Marlene was not empty – she was full – full of interior voices that she

84

felt the need to drown out. She didn't have anything in particular to say – simply, the sound of her voice drowned out the terrible things the monsters might say.

There is a line in *Jubilee*: 'As long as the music is loud enough we won't hear the world falling apart.' The same logic applied to Marlene's voice – as long as it was loud and insistent enough she couldn't hear herself falling to pieces. She just had to keep talking and shouting.

There is an old joke about people who talk a lot. Someone told it to Marlene. 'Do you know the 12-Step programme for people who talk a lot? On and On Anon!'

Marlene didn't laugh.

After one unfortune episode – for the sake of emotional balance certain nights, persons, events are best forgotten, or set aside in the place reserved for such toxic drama – Marlene went to a doctor who referred her to a therapist. He told her, regarding her ceaseless, sometimes noxious chatter, probably quoting from some book, 'Imagine that you have a child inside you who feels abandoned. This child feels that way because you are not considering his or her feelings. Every time you snare someone into listening to you talk for very long periods, it is as though you are abandoning this child again and again. You want someone else to take responsibility for this child, when he or she is your responsibility...'

Marlene put him straight, 'Listen the only kids I have in me, you fuckwit, are the dead ones – and I'm not paying attention to them, because they are talking fucking shit!' The consultation was over.

Afterwards, Marlene told the story and laughed. She often laughed. Her persona was that of the ever-up-for-a-giggle Cockney woman, complete with suitable slang, all delivered in flurries and streams of quick speech: 'Knock me down with a kipper missus if I'm tellin' you porkies. Nah, I 'aven't got any bees and honey, you berk.' And so on.

Her waving hands, blinking eyes, and her intensity mixed with cackling seemingly self-deprecating laughter. It was both fascinating – like she was transforming dead air into action – and really annoying all at the same time.

To people who hadn't regularly encountered her performance, Marlene seemed like energy on toast – give me two slices, make it three.

Robert liked to imagine that she entered the world kicking and screaming in frustration at having been cooped up for nine months. Because everything she ever did afterwards she did in a chaotic rush as if to make up for lost time.

She always came into the room at a run, the door somehow left on its hinges after she had crashed it open. Or, sometimes, after a few too many, she would stagger in. The booze acted as a de-accelerator, but she would make up for the loss in velocity by increasing the amount of gesticulation or the sheer pace at which she spoke.

Her normal everyday method of talking was akin to hellzapopin':
howareyadoing'mjustgoinoffroudnthecornerwanncom ewithorwha?

Robert, or others – especially if they were new to her sphere – would stare at her with a certain amount of incomprehension. She, meanwhile, would grow impatient, stamping her foot

'wellwassamattawidyacatgotachatonguei'mstandingro undlikealemonmayupyermindyer?'

The response was bemusement or laughter.

This would be answered in turn with the showing of a dirty pair of heels and the slamming of the door that would leave behind a vacuum.

She was like the Tasmanian Devil of Bugs Bunny/Daffy Duck cartoon fame. Communicating via slobbering growls, and indecipherable gibberish, its cyclonic motions ripped through trees, rocks and anything else that got in its way, while it searched for food. Marlene similarly worked a room. There were no survivors. You could run but you could not hide. Her favourite food was attention. Lots of it. Greedy Marlene.

Pandemonium followed her wherever she went. She was hard work, but someone had to do it – namely Robert. Don't mention Colin.

Once, in a huge farm loft in Amsterdam, there were perhaps 30 or 40 people trying to sleep after a big party. But Marlene raved and frothed all night exuding endless Mockney crap. At first there were sniggers and raised eyebrows. People tried to move away from her. Then they started throwing things. She maintained her wild spume of words with accompanying ticks and jerks like she was engaged in some low-level St Vitus Dance. In the end Robert had to drag her out of the room so people could get some sleep. She slumped. It was like the off switch had finally worked on a broken, erratic wind-up toy.

When Jack Kerouac said the only people for him were the mad ones, he was thinking of someone like Marlene, Robert joked.

Marlene loved the joke and laughed loudest. But she did not laugh last. Robert could see that future, of course.

In her mid-twenties Marlene's nature and behaviour was understood, dismissed and even encouraged by friends and associates as being punk rock, just having a laugh, or the result of too much speed and beer – good on you Marlene – or high spirits.

But as the years unfolded any high hopes that Marlene had ever had about stardom were dispelled in a future diminished – what had once been a wide open vista to traverse was now reduced to a thorny track leading to a blank brick wall – the kind of wall on which, decades previously, she might have spray painted No Future. Tragic in the proper sense, her face inflated like hot rubber by her meds, she was diagnosed with a variety of mental disorders.

The aspirations and joys of youth which she thought would insulate her from the terrible damage caused by time now raged in her.

Depression followed her like an invisible piss trail left by rats. She looked like, and had the demeanour of, a half-dissected rodent – cornered and still snarling in her own way; retreating into semi-professional victimhood, and seeking sympathy in a passive aggressive, self-pitying manner on Facebook – this became her real art. Marlene finally grew into the age – a well-matched narcissistic one where everything is focused via the prism of private sorrows and obsessions made public. She became an expert at openly wielding and capitalising on her helplessness.

This was existence as indulgence in specific and non-specific pain, tracing the trajectory of sentiment as far as could uncomfortably be taken.

Some people would say that they had known all along that Marlene was a raving nutcase. Some others just felt bad for her – a narcissist can be very charismatic and seductive. But Marlene didn't really know what to do with that power. Those people she attracted and gathered to her – my *dearest* friends – she later attacked in private as bores, fools, cretins and blockheads.

She cried and sighed: 'Oh God, why do these fucking people, these fucking boring fucked up imbeciles always talk to *me*? Always me! Me!'

Well, knock me down with a kipper.

One day in that distant future, a friend, Terry, asked Robert over coffee (Robert had long since given up booze), 'One thing that has always puzzled me – why did you get together with Marlene in the first place?' There was a pause. Robert thought of a particular line in the Kris Kraus novel *Torpor*, about a character, asked roughly the same question, 'Who sees her marriage as a love story summed up in three words: there was an emptiness. It frightened her. She tried to fill it.'

This was also Robert's answer.

Robert's friend Molly joined the conversation.

'Yeah that's what I don't do. It leaves me very alone, but hey.'

Molly, at a tender age, was self-possessed beyond her years.

'I know,' said Robert. 'You are self-aware. I wasn't. But I do have a character arc!' he laughed.

'It would be bleak if you didn't, wouldn't it!' Molly replied.

'A lot of people don't have character arcs at all, you might find in the future,' Robert said.

'Yeah, that's true,' said Terry.

9.

getting out of bed backwards

In Camden, after walking up St Pancras Way, Robert and Marlene started up their road – the flat was just less than half a mile away.

Right then, a rat or mouse crossed their path.

'Did you see that fucking horrible rat, or is it the acid?' asked Marlene.

'It was a mouse,' said Robert.

Marlene shrugged. 'It was brown.'

'It was pink,' said Robert, just to be confusing or because he wanted Marlene to, for no particular reason, believe he was still completely off the page.

He thought of Pinky, a young punk he knew who always dyed her hair that colour. One day, on the tube, someone remarked, within earshot, that it was stupid to dye your hair pink. 'What do you mean dye? I'll have you know I'm a natural pink,' said the young punk, and raised her skirt to expose pink coloured pubes. Pinky also had a white rat, whose fur she'd also dyed the same colour. The story was even written up in a punk fanzine. Pinky would die a decade or so later from cirrhosis. A shame she couldn't dye her pus yellow liver back to its natural pink.

Marlene started singing.

I saw a mouse!
Where?
There on the stair!

Robert stopped in his tracks. Marlene kept walking. Then stopped, too. She looked back.

Robert was also looking back. Memory whirled, mixing with dreams.

The first song he ever heard, or remembered hearing, was *A Windmill in Old Amsterdam* by Ronnie Hilton. He was 5, and the year was 1965.

The song's chorus may be familiar to connoisseurs of the ludicrous:

I saw a mouse!
Where?
There on the stair!
Where on the stair?
Right there!
A little mouse with clogs on
Well I declare!
Going clip-clippety-clop on the stair
Oh yeah

He heard it, standing looking up, agog maybe, or maybe not, at his parents' big old Fifties valve radio. He was in the small first-floor front room, hard grey and blue flecked linoleum on the floor, from where he could see his father's wardrobe. It was there that he kept his leather belt. The wardrobe door squeaked.

A little mouse with clogs on

He could also see part of his parents' bed. He didn't remember witnessing any Primal Scene, but you don't 'remember' these things usually. You need a Freudian therapist to drag it out, perhaps. The same way that Freud had plumbed the depths of one Sergei Pankejeff, a Russian aristocrat who, in the early 1900s, approached Freud to help him evacuate his bowels without the aid of an enema every time he wanted to go. What could have caused this blockage? The man recounted his childhood dream of being terrified by a group of white wolves sitting in tree. Freud interpreted this as the result of Sergei, or the Wolf Man, as he came to be called in psychoanalytic lore, having witnessed a Primal Scene – his father taking his mother from behind, like an animal. Robert thought: *If I was the Wolf Man I would have told Freud that the wolves were pink – just to see what he would have made of that.*

If Freud said that *the animal must be controlled* and Wilhelm Reich that *the animal must be freed*, Robert was definitely with the latter.

'Wilhelm Reich,' said Robert, in Agar Grove.

'Who?' said Marlene, her interest not particularly piqued.

'A bloke who understood a pink wolf when he saw one,' Robert replied.

'Fucking hippy,' said Marlene.

'It's colourful,' said Robert.

He was thinking: *if you are telling a story, and we all are all the time, then colour is the part of the narrative which lifts the tale from the mundane to the mythic. That's where you find the mysterious and the transcendent, if you're looking for it.* And Robert was looking hard.

Robert may or may not have witnessed a Primal Scene as a baby – Robert, with his acid-boosted powers of insight into the past and future, could feasibly have looked back to check, but the psychology of it all weirded him out. However, as a baby, he had definitely seen a real, large golly doll – 'real' as in something forged amongst the intricacies of consciousness or subconsciousness, which may have interested Mr. Freud, had he been consulted. It happened one night – doesn't it always? – when Robert awoke in his cot to find an actual pre-PC Robertson's jam figure – black, frizzy hair, the lot – staring at him through the bars of the cot. Robert looked at the figure. The figure looked at him. Then fear happened and Robert's screams sent the golly scuttling off to whatever elemental, ludicrous place it had come from. Maybe even across the landing to that first-floor front room, where stood the big radio. Robert, meanwhile, was taken into his parents' bed, sleeping between them. It was uncomfortable.

Robert couldn't imagine why the radio was even there, in the small front bedroom. His parents were not at all fond of background noise, and there was always too much work to do in those days – scrubbing, polishing, wiping, cooking, worrying, crying – to stop for simple everyday radio pleasures. But there it was, the big box of valves, trilling out its mild message, in the same room where Robert also saw, on another occasion, out of the blue, just like that, believe me, two or three large faces of old people in the curtains.

As a youngster, Robert didn't need acid to see things, it seemed. But then kids, before they are told what is possible and what is not, are often open to seemingly bizarre sights. The old people looked at Robert but remained silent. Their grey-haired heads looked down quizzically on him, a little boy, confused rather than scared by that which maybe shouldn't be, or should it? And then, startled by a thought process of disturbed logic – let's imagine another world within yet another world – he ran to escape and hid by a big cupboard near the landing.

Where?
There on the stair!

His mother, who had been busy scrubbing, polishing, wiping, cooking, worrying and crying, sensed that something was wrong. In later years, when Robert no longer lived at home, she would sense other disturbances from afar, knowing when Robert had been arrested, for instance.

On the day he saw the old people in the curtains, she came running up the stairs to save her son from the intangible. These things, memories or dreams, you carry with you.

Robert never did tell his mother about the old people, but she would have known them. They came from the same place as the stuff of the old Polish folk tales, fairy tales, she told Robert in his childhood. Tales which informed him that out there...

Where?

... strangeness and crazy magic were afoot. In her eastern Polish village, before being ethnically cleansed to Siberia by the Russians at the start of World War II, Robert's mother had herself seen the inexplicable lights lit by the village's agitated dead, encountered the devil's horses, and had been warned by her guardian angel about the many trials and, yes, tribulations to come.

Such tales, Robert thought, contain and maintain the unsettling rationale of broken dreams, in which nothing fits, and everything seems inescapable and imminent; and there are always bolts coming out of the blue; affirming that, really, we live in a fuzzy world far from the idea of anything that might be structured.

These same stories were also told to Robert by his *babcia*, or grandmother, who, some years later, climbed the stairs every morning with a cup of tea for her darling grandson.

Going clip-clippety-clop

One stair at a time, slowly, with difficulty, the tea in her shaking hand. Robert, her little prince, waited impatiently in bed, in the first-floor front room where he had years before heard *A Windmill in Old Amsterdam* and seen the old people.
Clip-clippety-clop on the stair

His grandmother's Parkinson's made the cup rattle against the saucer, spilling some of the tea. He would listen to this Parkinson's cup and saucer chatter, and wonder why she couldn't be a little more careful. And couldn't she be a little quicker about it? He was thirsty. In need of refreshment.

Such thoughts! In the same room where not only had he seen the old people in the curtains, but where he had also, many years earlier, gone into a dangerous

coma. His parents and a doctor gathered around the
boy's bedside, waiting for the ambulance when,
according to family lore, he sat up, pointed to a corner
of the room

Right there!

and asked: 'Who is the boy in white, the one getting
into the coffin?'
Thereupon, his fever broke and he came out of the
coma into normal sleep.

Robert was amazed by this peek into a half-
remembered dream world, on which it was hard to
focus beyond the edges and limits, zeroing into
something shimmering and centreless.

Robert was, through the years, convinced that he had
almost died, and that perhaps the old people had
intervened on his behalf. He had a double protection
line on his palm, he was informed by more than one
psychic he consulted.

After delivering the tea, much of it slopping in the saucer by now – tsk – Robert's *babcia* would remind him, warn him again: *never get up from bed backwards*. Never. Ever. Otherwise bad things would surely happen. For the rest of his life, Robert would heed that warning whenever he could – if he forgot or was otherwise distracted, he would feel slightly nervous for the rest of the day. This was just one of the superstitions with which the old peasant woman could easily transform the mundane into mystery, myth, and prophesy; spinning dark truths and, of course, untruths. These were her own ludicrous fairy tale songs to sing.

I saw a mouse!

Later, in 1978, Robert wondered if his grandmother, after her death that year, had joined the other old people in the curtains. Those people, Robert never saw again. Nor did he hear *A Windmill in Old Amsterdam* by Ronnie Hilton ever again after he heard it that first time – until Marlene sang it in Camden Town.

Well I declare!

10.

sleep meets with brief awakenings, repeatedly

Robert's mind flicked from the past to the future, like strands of his black dyed hair, in a shake of the head.

He saw himself standing in a room, looking at a framed photo.

He saw himself in the future looking at a photograph taken in the past of two young people, Robert and Marlene, grinning hard into a bright new tomorrow.

Robert looked at the picture, taken long ago, and thought: images can lie in many ways, maybe through manipulation or perspective. And, sometimes, over the course of time, he mused, the truth simply seeps out of a photograph like fine-grained sand from between two cupped palms. The smiles on the faces of these two people in the picture: me and her, her and me have

long since turned to grimaces frozen in a rictus of …
misery and boredom. Get the picture?

Robert looked at the couple in the picture, a Kodak
crack-up. Me and her, her and me. He didn't care about
them or her; he wanted to smash the photo to see what
was inside; to discover how it works, how the camera's
gaze had alighted and then moved on from this sacred
moment of reality, now so very unreal. In his reverie,
he dreamt an epic dream of an old house hit by a
tornado in slow motion. He looked on as millions of
minute particles of debris entered the abode through
the cracks in the windows and walls, sailing in, clouds
of it, to cover every single thing with a cold black dust
under which everything reverted to the namelessness
from which it came.

So very poetic, he said to himself.

A Catholic boy – he was a mindful ironist realising his
small reputation for debauchery and carnality would
be both enhanced and dimmed by the cultural and
psychological background of a punishing Catholic
upbringing – oh, that large dark framed picture of the

naked Jesus nailed to a cross hung above his parents bed – from Primal Scene to primal scream, and back again! But it was thanks partly to that Catholicism that Robert believed in the power of magic. At church, during his Confirmation, he was the only one of his group, dressed in his special Sunday best, who mouthed along with the priest's intonations, nodding at the relevant points, shaking his head at hellfire warnings, trusting implicitly in the Holy Ghost to propel him through life.

Having discarded the trappings of that religion in his very early teens, Robert retained faith in the ability of belief to effect change in the universe. So, every night in bed, he prayed, silently mouthing one hundred times, 'I wish he was dead. I wish Colin was dead. I wish he was dead,' etc. Visualising mayhem and breathing deeply, which always filled him with a sense of portent, Robert summoned supposed power from within, even though deep down, he knew that such dreadful thoughts would, rather than provide freedom from his malaise, bind him more tightly to the very pain he sought to escape. Yet, every day, he was mildly surprised that there was no announcement of Colin's death in a van crash, which is how he pictured the demise of the inveterate drink driver. But the good news never came, and Robert eventually abandoned his nightly prayers as mere wishful, and not particularly magical, thinking. But then magical thinking is often associated with grief, *a la* Joan Didion's my *Year of Magical Thinking*, and Robert was at this time already in mourning for his and Marlene's relationship.

Robert had been seduced and then overcome, not by Marlene, but by the comfort she offered for a while. He hated it when she went out. He wanted to stay in. And he knew that when people went out it wasn't because they wanted beautiful drugs, all-consuming blow jobs, exquisite below jobs, bewitching runny mascara, interactions/infractions with delicate people with magnificent minds and graceful sexual organs – 'the diamond grit of the night', as it were. It was because typically, they wanted to effect change in their lives to some degree, large or small. And Marlene wanted to go out all the time. This made Robert, the possessive prick, feel very uneasy. Robert wanted to stay in.

That made Marlene feel *fucking sick*. And tired. Sick of Robert who was holding her back. Why else wasn't she a *fucking star*? *Eh? Sick and tired of every fucking thing.* Sick of her face in the mirror (she had smashed many a mirror). Sick of the monsters. Of their voices. Of not being *a fucking star star star yet… oh stardust twinkle down on me*, she cried and wrung her heart in desperation nightly. She went out in her glad rags, but often forgot her hand bag, to see if she could attract *destiny*.

The lesson Robert had yet to learn and one that Marlene would never learn, perhaps, was that the truly magical way to get what you want is actually the opposite of the method they themselves were using – by employing not desperate magical thinking, but by adopting a magical *nonchalance*. By being cool, in other words. If you, first, affirm your desire and then forget about it and allow things come to you in their own time, they often will.

But what Marlene *had* learned, after a fashion, was that her experience of love, or a cheap approximation of that exalted feeling (Johnny Rotten had told her – via a music paper interview, but he was only talking to *her* – that love was not for humans) wasn't great. Taking it all into account, weighing everything up, it seemed clear the Eros hadn't exactly smiled on Marlene. Although, she hadn't particularly helped herself. The typical process for Marlene had been so far, so not good: initial animation about the idea that someone could restore her withered black heart – *oh, look what those monsters have done to me* – would be followed quickly by a sense of rage when the chosen person could not, or more likely would not, perform the impossible. And then that person, too, would become one of the Marlene's monsters who, she felt, had used and abused her. So, Marlene was always on the brink of outrage, full of impatience and hate – for everyone and everything that might have thwarted her. That this might merely be some person in the street, or in some club, who wore the wrong shoes or said the wrong things in the right way or the right things in the wrong way was by and by. Marlene, like most keenly judgemental people, was herself … arduous.

Robert knew that Marlene had the malevolent energy of deranged clowns, and that this energy was her mad muse. But he was still scared: of losing Marlene; of finding himself in the next unpredictable place. Where perhaps nothing would make sense, although yes, of course, certainly, nothing made sense then, at that time, either. He was not yet ready to repudiate the succour of degraded domesticity and answer the wild call of chance. He was not yet ready to say: 'Better to succumb in the roaring infinities than *this*.'

So, the poor fool held on to Marlene the way a man who thinks he's going to drown holds on to a heavy weight.

Really, what Robert didn't yet have was wisdom. Which, in the end, is really about trying to understand the complicated sense of arrangement between what drives a person and what could be called ethics and integrity – and that comes eventually by listening to your deepest self.

Marlene didn't have it, wisdom, because the voice of her deepest self sounded just like the voices of those monsters she was forever trying to blot out.

'We are what we regularly do,' that voice was trying to say. Marlene wasn't listening.

Marlene fucked people over. And she always overdid it, becoming objectionable.
This is what the voices reminded her of on a daily basis.

Meanwhile, Robert was always frantic and became pitiful.

'What are you trying to prove?' she said to him one day.

'That I love you. That you don't love me,' he said to her. As soon as he said it, he wondered why he had.

'Don't be so fucking sentimental, it makes me fucking sick. With your spotty chest, and always asking me where I'm going. Corny Polish cunt, ' she said.

There was no answer to that, really.

'But *of course* I love you,' she said to him straight away after her outburst, stroking his cheek and patting his head as she went out of the door.

Both were kidding themselves and kidding in general, or vice versa. Marlene was snide, but Robert was self-deluded.

There would be no big emotional or psychological marks at the end of this episode in Robert's life. But there would be growth and the vaunted character arc, which is the most important part of any story by far.

Robert, in Camden, looking to the future, laughed and thought about the unfolding story he was writing in his head – about how it would work on paper – and reflected: the thing about Marlene and her punk disdain for sentimentality: in reality it is the inability to be a complete human being – because being human is to sometimes be open and unafraid of the sentimental, the stupid and, yeah, the pitiful. About himself, he thought: when they claim you, the roaring infinites are never to be denied, never mind how hard you try.

Robert first knew that Marlene was cheating on him – although, really, he *knew* before – everyone always does – came after a weekend away with his mum – oh, young men rendered soft and inert by the love of their mothers.

The atmosphere at the flat had been verging on the evil for a while , and Robert's antenna had been up – clairvoyance in him was not triggered just by writing, or the peak experience of acid, or by proximity in that respect to a canal, which was something he himself imbued with the power of transmission anyway – neurosis would do the trick just as well. There is a story involving Joe Orton being tracked down by jealous boyfriend Ken Halliwell, who phoned Joe's publisher. 'How did he know you were here?' asked the publisher. 'They always know when they're in *that* state,' said Orton. Robert knew *that* state very well indeed.

One day, he found a strange stray blonde hair on the pillow case, but Marlene dismissed it, telling him that it was his imagination, even as he held the hair up in front of her. Magically, she managed to activate the internal process that caused him to negate the evidence before his very eyes: 'What are you fucking on about?

Shut up. You must be mad. A hair? I'll tell you what, you are hair brained. That is what you are.'

After another weekend away, he had come back to find a couple of beer cans on the table.

'Someone been over?' he asked.

'No,' she replied. 'I had a beer myself and then went to sleep.'

'Well, how come there are two cans?' he shook his head.

She laughed in his face. 'Why are you questioning me? I can't move for your fucking questions. You make me sick. You and your questions. And your spots. And your Warhol. But if you really want to know the truth...'

'Yeah,' he said.

'Actually, I had three cans, but I threw one away. And left two. That's why there are two cans. OK? Is that alright? You wanted the truth. Three cans. Two left.'

One morning, Marlene went to the corner shop to buy a newspaper. She never read papers, but there was a phone box by the shop. Quickly, Robert rang Colin's number – of course, he knew his number – and, yes, it was engaged. She returned without a paper and said that she was going out to meet a mate, a girlfriend.

'Who?'

'None of your beeswax!'

Certainly, even without the litany of lies uncovered, Robert knew. He knew even without, one day, pulling back the bed covers to find their bed messed up with dried sperm. Lots of it smeared everywhere. What a fucking mess. The swirls and dabs. The curlicue of old semen on black sheets, shouting copious joy and potency. An abstract painting of passion made by a maestro. But not by Robert. Marlene quickly whipped the sheets off the bed and told Robert he was fucking crazy, should be committed, to even think that anything untoward had happened. 'Fucking crazy idiot. You belong in a home. A loony bin.'

116

Robert began to think he was crazy, as though he was living in a Witold Gombrowicz novel, which is typically a map of extraordinary and portentous configurations and constellations that make absolutely no sense and offer no clue as to the reason behind *what is going the fuck on* – Kafka on bad speed – the systematic confusion of paranoia.

Robert would spend his time detecting things which have no logical connection, a discredit to the world of reality. *This is the stupid, disjointed experimental film that I have been waiting for the whole time, and in which I am now forced to act badly*, thought Robert. Nothing made sense. Robert was distracted and bewildered by the plot. He and Marlene both knew that Colin was the other character – but his part in the script was hidden from the role which Robert was playing. So it goes in these situations, of course.

Robert acted his part, but he did not *act* – like an archetypal, hammy Prince Hamlet he took no action. There was kids' stuff, tantrums and histrionics, some name calling, a bit of plate smashing, but if he had responded properly, confronted Marlene with the

117

standard him-or-me ultimatum, his world would have been turned upside down. The future would've then had to have been faced alone, a concept unthinkable and awful to Robert who, as a child, had told a school friend: 'You can't be lonely in this day and age – with TV, radio and music to keep you company.' Even as he spoke, Robert knew that reliance on impersonal communication might only affirm isolation. But, the fact he had voiced such an opinion revealed much about his fears.

Swaddled by his mother, and denuded at an early age of independence, he needed a partner who would fulfil lazy emotional needs. Someone who not only wanted him, but who would always be there someone who would save him – *Oh God, I can't do it on my own, I don't want to be on my own.* He was sceptical of the wider world, of his ability to survive and thrive within it, and of the bad decisions he might make. The world was one to fear, not to plunge into and explore and, though Robert was a person who advocated adventure, he secretly sought security. Without Marlene, he was surely doomed to a ghostly place. In short, Robert was scared of his own shadow. *Boo.*

He was also scared because he knew that there are key points – and they don't come often – when people can take a firm grasp of their own lives and change things around for the better. Robert thought he may have missed a big chance.

It sounds like Robert deserved everything he got. No one likes a tedious wet. But, really, all he lacked was a bit of insight. He had not yet learned that his greatest fear, loneliness, is not caused by being alone – rather, it is all to do with not having anyone with whom to honestly exchange ideas and thoughts with. You could be surrounded by a hundred people every day and still feel very lonely.

For all his fears, Robert would never end up being alone, yet there would be no escape from the feeling of loneliness – he never felt as though he belonged to this world. However, he did learn that the associated feeling of desperation could be alleviated and transformed into something positive by creativity, which is the magical process of giving something of yourself to the world.

But back then he thought, where do I go? Every way and path seems wrong.

So, he went nowhere with his unhappiness and did nothing. His life was one of compromise. Of fulfilment postponed. Of fantasy unformed. Of desire denied. Robert and Marlene still had clinical sex, and he thought of each orgasm as a small recompense for betrayal and humiliation. For, what he thought was a crushed soul. Really, his soul wasn't crushed in the slightest – it was just cringing in embarrassment.

Robert never thought of Marlene as ugly – or, if so, marked only by the kind of ugliness that suggested some puzzling spiritual deformity. And that may not have been entirely her fault. And it definitely didn't put him off wanting sex. It would take a lot to put him off that. There was a French girl with really bad breath and... but let's leave that in the past, or the future.

Meanwhile, the sex would suffice for a few days, until the pressure, both physical and emotional, built once more to a peak. Then, resigned, Marlene would get on all fours and proffer impersonal and cold, white buttocks.

The thinker William Gass had many a smart notion, but perhaps his best was the thought that we don't have the 'language which will allow us to distinguish the normal or routine fuck from the glorious, the rare or the lousy one – a fack from a fick, a fick from a fock.' Robert pondered this while mounting Marlene from behind and thought, *this is definitely a fock not a fuck*. Marlene unknowingly agreed. *Ah, what a fock up*.

Marlene also got on all fours for Colin. But she hated cocks. The passion of lovers was for dearth, as far as she was concerned. Hated men. And their stupid needs. It was like the scene in the *Great Rock and Roll Swindle* in which a critic with flies on her face, modelled on Julie Burchill apparently, says, channelling Valerie Solanas and SCUM: 'You, Steve Jones, are nothing but a walking dildo doing a good plumbing job. You'd swim through a river of snot, wade nostril deep through a mile of vomit, as long as you thought there was a sexy cunt at the end of it – and those cunts! Daddy's girl! Daddy's girls are in awe of the Sex Pistols! They really believe that what they're grooving to bores them to shit! Daddy's girls are just hot water bottles with tits.'

Well, Marlene was a daddy's girl – but her daddy had died and left her and, worse, was now saying shit things to her in her head, like in some cliched script written by someone with an imagination deficiency.

For Marlene, every fuck was a compromise fuck, just a demonstration of options – she never really enjoyed it unless she was utterly off her head. Giving blow jobs was a trade-off – illustrating that in some relationships, the act raises questions of who, exactly, is the real sucker.

Colin. Or, as Robert named him: 'Colin the Wanker.' Or, simply 'the Wanker'. Robert would not call him by his real and given name, would not dignify him, would not admit the humanity of his rival. To Robert, Colin was not a person, more a dismal entity sent by forces dark and dangerous to cause havoc and mayhem in the lives of good people such as himself. If, for the purposes of dehumanisation, Robert could have given him a number instead of a nickname he would have. But, 'the Wanker' would suffice for the time being.

Robert's friend Terry called his own love rival 'the Mollusc.' 'I came in the other night and the Mollusc was sitting in the front room with his trousers round his ankles,' said Terry, detailing his live-in girlfriend's affair.

In fact, Marlene had become close to Colin after he had confided in her about his own girlfriend's wayward wanderings. In response to these, Colin had exacted an utterly psychotic physical and psychological revenge – a nasty piece of work, by anyone's standards. But if Robert could have accepted him as a person, not simply as a bad smell, he could have asked him, 'Hey, Colin, what name did you call your girlfriend's lover boy?'

There is a telling piece in Henry Miller's *Sexus* where, having unsuccessfully fought against his partner's infidelities and brazen lies, Miller is forced to pretend that everything is okay. For this, he receives a pat on the head, like a good dog, one who wags his tail in appreciation of being allowed to come in from the cold

123

by a woman who has become the master of his fate. At the end of the book, the first part of the *Rosy Crucifixion* trilogy, the canine Miller howls his capitulation. Robert, too, silently howled, the inside of his skull echoing with despair, like the sound of an amplified outburst of static. It was a terrible noise – just like Marlene's monsters – but one which blissfully blocked out even more terrible thoughts, enabling him, the great inaction hero, to continue to exist while trying to slow down time; to decelerate the solid lurch of the fearful and unstoppable future.

Robert was looking at himself looking at photograph of two young people, Robert and Marlene, grinning hard into a bright new tomorrow.

He will in the future think: *this story is an ode to growing pains of eternal children*.

He will think: *this story is about gaining the wherewithal to write your own narrative.*

The story is about attaining the capacity and joy of moving on, and of keeping on moving.

11.

speed is frozen

Robert, in Camden, was still looking into the future, and saw himself in a few years' time.

He was living in Camberwell, in south east London. Robert and Marlene were no longer living together, but they were still a couple. Or, pretending to be. Marlene – she had still not achieved stardom – *fucking cunts all of them* – was also seeing Colin. She lied to Robert about doing so. And he pretended to believe her in order to maintain the status quo – he *still* wasn't ready to face the world entirely on his own.

He lived with friends in a big house in Camberwell – a much more free and expansive place than Camden, he felt. He loved the openness and possibility for interaction on offer there. Comparatively, Camden was claustrophobic bedsit land. Camberwell could sometimes, at least, be rinsed in sweeps of allure –

Camden was mostly sullen and a little sinister. In Camberwell, Robert played music, read books in the nearby Ruskin Park, wrote for the music papers, took speed, cycled around, saw girls and went about the tricky business of activating the next phase of his life – *this* was far more arousing than the simple search for sex.

He hooked up with Marlene most weekends, to take speed.

Other times, Robert was left to his own debauched devices.

Robert in Camden watched himself in the future in Camberwell, sitting at his desk writing in a large blue diary. He looked over his own shoulder and saw these words, about a drug experience, being written by himself:-

Diary entry 5 June 1988: I tremble and wonder as I cut up some speed. Fix some water in a spoon and mash the mixture into a dangerous solution. Add a piece of fag filter to trap the clag and draw up the watery drug into

the needle. Slowly to avoid air bubbles but not quite
succeeding and not quite fucking it up enough to start
again. Flex my arm with a guitar strap and decide on a
thin but prominent vein. Slide the needle in and draw
blood – I'm in! Inject the drug, but in my fear of a
beginner I shake the needle out of the vein and a bulbous
blue swelling arises. I stop in time and start the whole
ritual again. On the other arm choosing the big vein. I
hear it pop and see the blood and taste the exhilaration
as I again, shakily, push the plunger home. There's no
real buzz, but I pace the room and smoke fag after fag
and find the Johnny Thunders record and play Looking
for a Kiss*. For a junkie Thunders plays pretty good*
amphetamine accompaniments. Feel panicky about not
getting a big rush, not really exploding with the drug
and dab a whole lot more. And off to meet people at the
Cambridge. I am affable and interested. Discharging the
night with my spunk into a girl. But where is mention of
my career success? My creativity? My financial spirit?
Nowhere. Elsewhere in a parallel universe. Not here.

Home next day to read Kentucky Ham*. A tale of an A*
head jerked out of his self-destructive, needle fixed
lifestyle by the authorities and his rehab through work

127

and exertion. I liked the bit where he had four days to go
before a deadline and went off the straight and narrow
narrative bunging in crumby half-baked quarter
thoughts. The book is real, even if as a train of thought
it's rubbish – just like this diary.

Robert, in Camden, was able to see his future self
writing about himself in his diary *and* those events
being written about, all at the same time. Quite a trick.

But watching himself in this way didn't detract from
the concrete composition, depiction and understanding
of the scene. It hit Robert like a smack in the eye – or,
rather, speed in the eye. Robert's gaze was not at all
detached or diluted by time's unfathomable distance.

He thought: it is beautiful but repugnant – and banal, of
course. He wished he could take a photograph – the
scene might make a good book cover. Art in the
aesthetic sense – taut, narcissistic, sinuous, glam and
sexual, focused on a silver otherness. Art that
challenged perception of, at source, disappearance,
nothingness. Art and speed – the underground,
underworld pallor and pose of decadence. Robert, in all

his temporal positions, was something through which that idea passed.

I need a fix and a kiss
I need a fix and a kiss
I need a fix and a kiss
I been looking for a kiss

Robert thought: *I am not looking for a fix. I want* be *fixed. The Dolls weren't singing about drugs at all – they were singing about fucking redemption.*

Robert had never seen himself concentrate on something so intensely as when putting the point of the needle to its target. The vein reminded him of the Camden canal, snaking and foreseeing a future. He thought about the serenity at that very point – *what's the point*? The lack of an initial rush did not surprise him – somehow that lack was apt in context of the aesthetic: distant but electrified. There, in that pressurised gap between desire and insouciance was located the sense of cool that Robert had always cultivated and projected – like a film: *noir. But,* he wondered, *is there anything human here*?

Robert watching the scene and himself write about it felt as though he was blurring the line between observed and sensed experience. Amaranthine time. He felt the heartbeat – at the speed of the clock, the speed of his cock, the speed of speed. Context abridged within place and time. Cool collapsed, emotions within amplified imagination. Reclining into the deterioration, digging the vein, digging the/a girl – or, thought of the/a girl. Elegant cold gratification in nothing – but the deep interest in a strangeness of which, in the howling infinites, we are constituted.

Diary entry 11 June, 1988. Saturday and fucked myself up – and fucked Marlene after licking her arsehole and the join of her buttocks and back as though it was her clit. The speed dampened me and I became hard in her very hot cunt before fucking her. The sex isn't as full of wild abandon as it used to be – soon there will be nothing left for us.

Terry talked about girls, Carol – how he'd had trouble with relationships and sex, nothing in bed, how it wouldn't happen for him.

Ray – impotence.

Everyone I know seems to get it together only now and then.

Diary entry 18 June, 1988. The speedy pseudo interest in everything and everybody. The self-assurance. The confidence. All false – shattered by the coming of dawn.

Ah and the lust –I just wanted to stick my cock in the cutie with the black dress – her cunt, mouth and arse. Made do with Marlene. I stick my cock in her mouth and she bites it, I suck and chew her nipples for ages while holding a handful of her hair. Stick a tennis racket up her cunt and finish her off by flicking my tongue over her open cunt while she wanks and licks my asshole. Deep deserved sleep follows. Marlene has to get up early. I sleep and stay in bed until three.

Diary entry 25 June, 1988. At someone's house. We put the double sofa bed out in the front room . Got some alcohol from Graham. Marlene talked to me for ages with speed exhilaration. I listened with speed induced

interest. Passing comments and adding opinions.
Marlene asked me not to launch into fucking too quickly
and to let it come. I held onto her toes, stroked her legs.
Then moved onto her tits and actually got her moaning
with pleasure. Shock. Moved down to her cunt and licked
that but not for too long. Back to her tits which I fucked
with my cock. Shoving it in her mouth. Finally getting it
in her cunt and riding her. We talked pantingly about
how she'd treat a girl. Would she suck her cunt and arse?
Yes. Moan. Do I know such a girl? Yes. Would you piss on
her? Yes – would you like me to piss on you? No, but I'll
piss over your tits and never mind the carpet! She laid
herself on the floor as I tried to get the shower to flow.
No luck (not getting it up is one thing – but this was the
first time not being able to piss! Never happened before,
honest). I put an empty vodka bottle into her cunt and
went to drink some water. But tired of piss inaction she
leapt up stood astride me and let it flow. Smearing her
piss over my chest. My turn came, I sat astride her and
between her gasps of excitement I splashed her tits. She
grabbed my cock and directed it onto her nipples. She
looked shy, aghast and exhilarated at the same time.
Afterwards I told her she looked like a shy whore. I took
her by the nipples and led her to the bed where I fucked

and her mouthed more lesbian fantasies as she
shuddered and came. I pushed her legs back over her
head so that her legs rested on her shoulders and fucked
her hard. Her hand fondled my bollocks. I came in gouts.
Sleep was sound. Morning – jovial references to pissing.

The film of these scenes would be full of faces, shot in relentless close-ups – all margins and edges; her: tweaked repression; him: unclenched urgency.

Robert, the one being secretly observed by himself, felt weird: like he was being haunted. There was definitely a presence. He had a sense of foreboding. There was a ghost here: a ghost of a chance.

Robert, the observer, believed, like Jacques Derrida, that that the future was full of ghosts – it belonged to ghosts – to the apparitions and those they haunted with their images.

Robert looked at the scene, and thought it was unusual for Marlene to be so present and so intensely immersed. Typically, he thought of Marlene as someone who, by being part of the pre-porn generation, had missed her natural milieu. She was someone who hated sex with men so, *a la* the porn generation, was happy to be fucked any way you/they liked, faking it just like she faked everything: with a rabid vigour – especially her orgasms. She made those into a celebrity/star event, but felt nothing. Like porn, this performative sex was boring – although Marlene treated it as a useful rehearsal for the wider empty spirited performance, on which the function of stardom, and the craving for it, is based.

She would stop having sex relatively early in life after hopes and dreams of even any approximation of stardom had finally been discarded. Colin, who she married, didn't care – it wasn't his thing either. When someone asked her why she married him, Marlene said she needed a new father – someone who would look after her without hurting her feelings. Without saying shit things to her. Like every *fucking* body had, *every fucking cunt has*. What a mess.

Robert thought the scene would also make part of an interesting film. Warhol – of course – came to mind.

Robert thought, flippantly, his balls could be like Andy's silver helium balloons – made by Andy so he could watch his career floating away, although of course, it didn't. Robert would offer his balls as a statement of intent – of the auteur, someone with an awareness of his own gestalt rather than just his output . He might paint them silver. Or, write a message on them – in small text, on which the camera would zoom, left and right respectively: 'nothing' and 'emptiness'.

The camera would focus on the scene in mute fascination.

The irony would be seen in Marlene kissing those balls. Marlene who wanted so desperately, more than anything, to be Edie Sedgewick. She empathised with her fucked-up daddy issues – Edie had famously walked in on her adulterous father in bed with a girlfriend and, for her trouble, was slapped by daddy who told her in no uncertain terms that *she did not see what she saw*. Edie's father also made advances on her. Marlene wanted to step into Edie's persona: skinny, stylish, beautiful, cool, rich, a superstar for the sake of it, and in love with self-destruction – all of which, apart from the latter, was unattainable and impossible for her.

Robert felt that he would like to stand, watch and film Marlene as she destroyed herself – with drugs, resentment, jealousy, hate, self-loathing, crime, and self-pity. He would not help, just record the story as it unfolded – his aloof creativity would excuse him from accusations of callous exploitation. Yes, just like Andy.

Robert thought, this film is about art, sex, and speed. And time. The skinny: picture and action streams and leaks, visual isolation curious enthrallment beyond image and attraction – subverted and fixed hallucination – imagined literal time – temporal senselessness and helplessness created by the meaning: sorry, some other time –frustration carnal and obscene: poetry. Yeah.

Robert had it all worked out. A sure fire hit.
The theme of voyeurism, and meditation on same, was a given. Robert, storyteller and self-described auteur, would while watching, not miss a single detail.

Robert finished watching both himself writing about the scene and the scene itself, and concluded: 'My vision and my cock were always clean – what more can anyone ask for?'

12.

the animal must be freed

In Camden, Robert saw himself at the end of the decade, in New York.

Nat Finkelstein's unpublished autobiography, *14 Ounce Pound*, begins with Nat sitting in a prison cell talking to the ghost of his dead father. Nat tries to explain and justify why and how he ended up behind bars (in fact, drug smuggling in Paris); how he traipsed for years around the dusty corners of the globe 'on the run' from US authorities who he believed had put out a 'dead or alive' on him – in fact, this may not have actually been fact – *para-fucking-noia Nat*; how he had been done bad by Andy Warhol; and how he had then taken revenge on the middle class fools, fakes and soft heads, which is also how he viewed the Warhol milieu, by selling drugs – Al Aronowitz described him as, 'Nat Finkelstein, Kokaine King of Woodstock.' The reader isn't told what Nat's dead dad thought of all this. Perhaps he gave him a stiff talking to.

Robert read this work-in-progress while staying with Nat in New York over the summer of '89. He'd interviewed him in the Spring about his book *Andy Warhol: The Factory Years*. He inscribed it: 'To Robert, remember the cry of the mutant, "I need creatures who resemble me."' And then kept ringing him to insist he go stay with him in the States – the mutant obviously thought Robert was his kind of creature.

Robert loved that book. A fantastic collection of pictures and memories of the Silver Factory during Finkelstein's tenure as unofficial resident photographer between 1964 and 1967. A chronicle of speed, madness and fabulous art, full of speed freaks, hustlers, junkies and geniuses; recalibrated fantasies about instant celebrity (Nat, by the way, thought Edie was an idiot), money, decadence and rock 'n' roll (Nat's picture featured on the back of the first Velvet Underground LP). Robert's kind of scene.

Nat lived in a tiny first apartment a few blocks across from the East Village. No kitchen. Not even a kettle. If you wanted a coffee, you went downstairs and across the road to the deli. Nat slept in the living room, on a fold out sofa. Robert was in a little annex, with just about room enough for a single bed. When he was with girls, Robert had to go to theirs'. There was no other furniture, and Nat had no possessions to speak of. A suitcase. Some documents – his work-in-progress – and a bunch of old negs (treasure), all just piled up on the floor. A tape player with a couple of cassettes – *London Calling* and *The Velvet Underground* (Robert and Nat discussed which was best – Nat's theory: Brits always went for *VU*, Americans, including himself, the Clash. Yeah, Robert went for *VU*). Nat later topped up this sparse collection after someone he vaguely knew jumped out of the window at the Chelsea Hotel – they went up to the poor soul's room to rifle through his things – so it went in these hurried visits to locations of despair and violence.

There was also a telephone at Nat's. But no one ever rang.

By the turn of the century, art, music, and cultural output of various hues has been flattened and marked down for fast turnaround; packaged, bundled up, repackaged again to satisfy the need for product and the media's requirement for subject matter: boiled down into palatable mulch.

Nat, via his intimate association with Warhol and VU (who he called: 'The psychopath's Rolling Stones'), would, if he had lived, be clamoured over for exhibitions, appearances, interviews, work, rights, prints sales, adverts, the whole shebang.

But in 1989, pre-cultural acceleration, no one really wanted to know. The mutant largely cried in vain.

The phone also never rang because Nat wasn't a particularly well-liked man. He was garrulous, argumentative, gruff, unreconstructed and didn't tread lightly on anyone's sensibilities.

Moreover, he didn't look the part. At the Factory, a world inhabited by beautiful if disposable wild boys and girls, Nat – a small, balding, old-looking schlub –

lowered the tone. Lou Reed said, 'The three worst people in the world are Nat Finkelstein and two speed dealers.' Nat was expelled from the Factory paradise when he dared suggest to Andy that they collaborate.

In 1989, Nat was regarded in a similar fashion by the NY Club Kids, whose energy he tried to tap by photographing them in clubs like Red Zone, World, Save the Robots et al.

Robert hung out with some of the cooler Clubs Kids, the girls in big platforms, walking to the Chelsea, telling the drug dealers to fuck off.

The Kids, led by future murderer Michael Alig (one of the most truly empty people Robert ever met) tolerated Nat, but only barely, because he had a camera – of course, exposure was something the Kids craved even more than the ketamine and E that fuelled the scene.

The phone remained silent.

But there was a lot to like about Nat, apart from when he had just been freebasing (a former addict, he hadn't quite lost his love of coke at that time).

These were days of E and coke – speed was infra dig and unavailable outside of a bathtub in the Midwest, something Robert was a little sad about.

Yes, Nat was bitter and whiny about his lack of acclaim and respect, but he was also honest about the part he played in his own downfall and stasis via the dismal drugs 'n' crime process.

It was in New York, and via Nat, that Robert finally learned and assimilated the big secret about ambition, creativity and career.

Nat taught him that, well, all considered, in truth, everything flows away sooner or later in an ephemeral kind of way – it is better to shine within the moment, perhaps; to fully fill one's boots and be true to your own nature rather than lick the world's arse.

Robert never forgot and never looked back.

Nat was also courageous – when one of the gang was mugged for his sunglasses outside the opening of a new club on the borders of Alphabet City Nat didn't hesitate in throwing his fair share of punches – he was old school Brooklyn tough. He was funny with it. The writing in the version of *14 Ounce Pound* that Robert read was a little sentimental and maudlin, but his words in *The Factory Years* cut to the quick with a hilarious edge.

Of course, Nat embodied all the acerbity and anguish of the city. His world was tainted with an isolating sense of melancholy, pungency and the fidgety foreboding that it was all going to end in salty tears. But he remained an insouciant outsider following his own crazy rationale – the ambiguous somewhere between elation of expectation and the riddle of failure. And he did it very bluntly, which, again was funny – it was a guffaw in acknowledgement of the mad persistence that keeps everyone all hanging on despite the knocks.

The trip climaxed with a night for Nat's book at the Red Zone club, 440 W 54. The flyer and poster listed those luminaries who organiser, Club Kid Susan Anton, had invited to the event – Betsey Johnson, Coca Crystal, Steve Maas, Herbert Hunke, Mary Woronov, David Dalton, Henry Connell (*Interview*), Gregory Corso and... Robert!

When the summer was over, Robert saw himself return from New York filled with a sense of possibility and the future.

13.

tongues - not giving but speaking

Back in the past, Robert scratched his spikey head.

'What the fuck is that?' he said, looking out of the window.

He and Marlene were in their tiny room in a housing association house in West Hampstead. Before their move to Camden, they shared this house with Robert's friend Terry, a drug fiend called Ziggy and a couple of wannabe fashion designers. Everyone in this scene was a wannabe of sorts – wannabe journalist/writer, rock star, etc. Although, they told themselves, and took pride in the assertion, that unlike, say, the similarly disposed New Romantics they weren't trying to climb up the greasy ladder. They, the last punks, the positive punks, the hippy punks, the true punks, didn't want to ascend the ladder, they wanted to kick it down. They were not careerists, they said. In truth, most would clamber over their crippled auntie to get up that ladder.

Robert and Marlene had been out briefly to the Tribe Club, or it might have been the Batcave, but had left very early.

'What?' said Marlene.

'*That*!' exclaimed Robert, pointing into the night.

'What?'

'Look!'

Marlene joined him at the window and looked at his pointing finger – she clearly had not come across the Zen analogy: 'A finger pointing at the moon is not the moon.' Neither had Robert but he had seen *Enter the Dragon*, in which Bruce Lee pretends to be wise by ripping off that snippet of Buddhist teaching: 'Don't think. FEEEEEEEL! It's like a finger pointing away to the moon. Do not concentrate on the finger or you will miss all of the heavenly glory!' Bruce is very kindly

147

instructing someone about the importance of staying fully present in the moment. Not drifting off. Drifting off was one of the things that both Robert and Marlene were good at, but not on this night.

'Do you see it?' asked Robert.

'What?' said Marlene, getting a little irritated.

'*That*!' Robert gestured with his finger. '*That*!'

What Robert saw in the night sky – *that* – could be most easily described as a UFO. But it wasn't a flying saucer in shape, it wasn't some obscure light in the sky that could be practically anything, it wasn't a cylinder, or a triangle – both common UFO shapes – it was more like the freaking Mothership. It looked like a huge ocean liner floating in the sky, one that could accommodate thousands of people. Or beings. It was marked by rows of brightly lit portholes, from which these beings were, doubtless, Robert imagined, looking down on *him*. It moved slowly, almost imperceptibly so, across the sky, not too high, not too low. No one could miss this, thought Robert.

Finally, Marlene looked up.

'Do you see it?' Robert asked.

Marlene didn't answer, her jaw dropped open. It took something very unusual to stop Marlene talking. Her stunned silence confirmed to Robert that he was not just seeing things. Or, that they had a shared vision, perhaps.

Robert loved UFOs. He thought they were vehicles for, or expressions of, so-called beings of light or angels or whatever people liked to call these entities. People who have experienced contact with these beings often report that they talk gibberish about existence, time and purpose – exactly the type of stuff that philosophers/deep thinkers talk nonsense about every day, to be fair. Robert wondered: *is it really all gibberish or is it a message from cosmic central that we can't grasp?* Yeah.

It was at that very moment that Robert himself started talking. He couldn't stop himself.

He was leaning on the window sill, looking so intently at the UFO as it inched and crawled across the sky, and what he said was like something that was unfolding unedited in his mind, a big imaginative unfiltered, unarranged sweep of language unfixed in context – in other words, Robert started talking complete and utter gibberish.

'Where am I? Like a million miles away and a million light years more. Where the dear roam. I want to take another drink and then drink some more. Where the fuck is this going? Down, down to the underground. But what's the command? Between science-dogma and sado-politico-religious hegemony, there's nowhere to run, never mind hide. Except here.

'Trying to avoid a big world sweep. It's not just money – it is your soul; all time control. *That* is the real energy which makes this mother ship work, it's all in the mind, right? Talk about a void before and behind. Mama, we're mental now. Cutting across and beyond righteous ritual , conditioning or even fear. The neural sensitive imprint in the brain is an addictive. It leaves you wanting more and more and more. More soul food, more sold food, more satisfaction. And the direction: express elevator up – to nothing. To the scaffold. But no direction at all because there is no reason to find anything, especially yourself. Because you wake up

'Feeling like someone different every day. An automatic writing for the big programme. What is more, the holy sacrament is, like DNA, inconclusive. Behind and before, no future in the universe's dreaming. A loaded grease gun stuck up time's ass. Out into space – the space and pattern between worlds where there's no big barrier, only pretty funny ugly shapes, stretching out, feeling and ticking. A little bit of automatic bonus – some more satisfaction. But it's all pseudonometry. A foamy war; the creation of a wave – silver like gold, except this serpent shines without glittering. Year in year out and in again. That is the rhythm; relentless like an old pig iron auto-hammer smashing down into thin invisible air for a millennium or two. Nothing but the hammer. No friction, no burn for anyone, behind and before. Free for all. Except for the world's forgotten boy. A street walking cheater. Intravenous Venus on a half shelf life. Why did I reject it? There must be six hundred and sixty six reasons. What the fuck, it didn't take in my head. And I was left to circumnavigate the orb, lots, lost and lonely. Looking for a kiss and a fix. Well, I'll fix it in the mix. Always. Cause I was the only one who had a reason for reason and the will to go about it. Yes, I had the smarts. A calling.

'And for money I will sell holy artefacts – a tea towel on which Elvis, an old time saint, is naked in all his glory, holding just his guitar, or an Elvis bedside clock where he winks, belches and slurs the words to his hymn *Old Shep* as you wake up.

'Yes, I was looking right into the eye of a tuneless moon when something fucking strange happened. A sister went weird on me – a freeze blank look in her eye, above and beyond the usual. Like she was possessed, not herself, although she and everyone else never is or are. She was spitting the most unusual little sayings which I was quick enough to write down. Man, the stuff – "I am the axle of the wheel and the cube is the circle" and "listen to the numbers and the words: 4 6 3 8 A B K 2 4 A L" and so forth and so on until there was enough mystery and history to fill a medium sized tome of 77 pages. Well I was a dog agog and when she finished she just sat and blinked and looked. She was the same and not. Only I could tell the difference. It was in her engine. Her brain. I knew that she was no longer on automatic. I was scared. One thing's as certain as the diamond glint crease in Elvis' pink peg slax, that big jumble of words was a revelation. A key. A weapon. And I was sure that the message was in the medium, the psychic. It was in the rhythm, a preternaturally constructed code to switch on or off, depending on how you look at it. So this was the reason why I was the world's forgotten boy. And now I knew, I blew. As far as I was concerned, this scene was as anti-life as a tube of lube on the extra quick. Utopia could wait! I could just about live on napalm dust economy. But then Crazy Time took a turn again. One hot evening, she spun brightly with only the fear light to guide her, telling things as they should or shouldn't be. I think my Holy Guardian Angel was talking. Strung out on lasers and climbing the chimney stacks along 22 paths that lead to right here and now.

'The angels flew, still gold but tarnished. Ready to storm the gates of heaven itself. As if I would! And now my Holy Guardian Angel informed me it was time to dry and fly and die, or all three. No time to adieu the vision or the voice. An erupting puzzle of periodical and cyclical amazement. I was Angel food. And it must have been something I ate. I woke up.

'The room was full of napalm smoke. It floated vertically like a wrong side wire. There windows but there were bars of flame across them. Which was bad. I think I had seen the room in my dreams before. The napalm smoke irritated my throat. So I called out: "Fire!" The door opened and a man jumped in. there were wings where his arms should be. He looked around, and asked: "Where?" "Down below," I answered. He laughed. "Where am I?" I asked. "Exactly where you should be," he said. "We all are." This made sense, at last. It was all adding up. He went out. The door shut. The place I am speaking about is in 22 places, and none of them are called 'home'.

'So that was the real nature of things. It was just business. You don't have to be clinical or cynical about it. You can spend your life fighting it, but your finger's always on the fast forward of desire and disaster. So here I am watching a heap of naked bodies falling

154

through infinite space. Coiled heretic visions. Supra-
Beatnik dreams – we are all Lucifer, aren't we? Jerking
at the flailing of useless limbs and tensely contorted
musculature as the disempowered drop sheer down
into the void.

'Huh, I prefer 1960s chrome – all Sputnik red. Spunking
up the night sky with voluptuous bearings – due east
bright, sad star. But at the end I knew I would say: "I
was cured." And this time I would mean it. Although
there is no escape – instead a chiasmus – hell within
me, within me: hell. Divine rhetoric. Like I was some
Icarus, Prometheus, Faustus, Johnny Thunders – or any
of those people like Lesley Winer who says: "Words I
have none, I just steal them to make them talk. I know
they're stolen but I don't give a fuck." I don't either.

'I just need a drink. Why does everything have to be so
extreme? Why are they feeding me this dim star in
isolation with nerve endings feedback-black like
chrome that had been singed in a car wreck. Then
maybe madness is what is all comes down to. The
reason for all the ritual and the rightness, evocation
with the aid of Evo-Stickschtick, gluing and pounding

155

together all the crazy parts that add up to the hole. Where live all the Gods and dogs with their faceless faces and un-nameable name calling. Here at last I can reclaim my own freaky daemon. Like a falling star. Like paradise lost. That's where I am.'

Robert stopped talking. Then a long pause.

'Is that a beatnik thing? A beat poem?' Marlene asked – she'd hardly been listening, but she caught a few phrases. 'I think I can nick some of that for something.'

The UFO finally disappeared out of Robert's (and Marlene's) sight line.

Robert then said: 'What the fuck was that?'

He looked around, at Marlene and the small room, decorated with his *Anarchy in the UK* poster, and a picture of Patti Smith, and added, 'What the fuck is *this*?'

Gives you a real lift. For closer harmony.

14.

nothing fits and everything seems imminent

Back inside the Camden flat Robert and Marlene were safe but still unsound – a fresh and strong wave of acid swept over them, sending the couple reeling into the bedroom.

The voices started chattering hard in Marlene's head. *Yadda yadda yadda.* On and on. If you've got nothing nice to say, say nothing – that's what Marlene's dead dad always said – so she didn't speak to him for a year. Now, she repeated the saying to him: *if you've got nothing nice to say, then shut your fucking big ugly mouth, dad.* But he would not be silent.

So, Marlene was almost glad when Robert started to unbutton her original Sex shirt, from the Kings Rd shop – if you're going to call a shop Sex and put the name up in big pink rubber letters it's pretty clear that you're really more interested in making a statement than in sex – and this was echoed by many of those who wore the clothes, including and especially Marlene. She hated sex, but made Sex and Seditionaries clothes her *raison d'etre. Johnny Rotten wore a fucking bondage suit.* It was a religious experience. Marlene had bought the clothes up like they were going out of fashion, which they were – in the late 70s and very early 80s, when punk had finished and no one wanted the clothes anymore, you could buy them on the cheap. Marlene would wear the clothes until she could no longer fit in them – whereupon she would store them in a suitcase for ever and ever. Hidden, like her.

Robert thought, craft must have clothes but truth loves to go naked, which was the slogan graffitied behind that big pink Sex sign, and continued to strip Marlene. She was glad because even though she hated Robert and his stupid thick cock, sex might distract her from what the voices in her head were saying – *fucking shit cunts.*

'Let's lie down,' said Robert. By which he meant 'Let's fuck,' of course.

159

Marlene could hear his cock harden. It sounded... hairy.

'Ooh, that acid,' she gasped.

Any stimulant, no matter how weak – he had to be careful with strongly brewed tea – made Robert want to have sex. With the acid pulsing through him, his lust was off the scale. He hurried and fumbled with various buttons, zips and straps – fucking bondage trousers – the strap was always getting in the way when you least need it to – running away from Teds and other idiots in the past, fumbling in bed these days.

Marlene, meanwhile, lay back and allowed herself to be undressed completely. She had to admit, the acid was giving her a little tingle, too. The nakedness, the openness, the saliva, the mess – it usually made her sick, but the acid made it almost bearable.

She looked at Robert – saliva was falling from his mouth in anticipation, it seemed to her. Streams and globs of it hanging from his open, leering mouth. The dirty fucker, she thought.

Robert took his own clothes off quickly. Marlene looked at him. Black hair. Sometimes it was red, or another colour, sometimes it was blonde – but not for ages – she was glad because that would have clashed with Colin. Two blondes – too much! She insisted that Robert dye his hair black. *Now, they were salt and pepper.* If she had ever been into having a threesome with the two of them, which she never was, *God fucking forbid, one at a time is too much,* it would at least have looked aesthetically balanced. But, Robert's hair looked longer, she hated long hair – fucking hippie.

She looked more closely at him, and recoiled. Not only was his hair too long, it looked like it had spread down his chest and back and, well, every fucking where. Robert had a pelt! His build was more powerful now, had he been down the gym? His forehead was wide, *Jesus his jaw looked strong*, his nose was blunt. *Christ.* She rubbed her eyes. His ears were relatively small and triangular and the limbs long and robust, with comparatively small... paws! *Robert has turned into an animal. He had turned into a fucking full-on wolf!*

161

And did that make her Little Red Riding hood? Of course it did.

Robert sighed a little – but to Marlene it sounded like a series of growls, barks, and whines. *As long as he didn't start fucking howling – let's think of the neighbours here.*

Robert wanted her from behind, on her knees. Of course he did. He tapped her flank. Marlene liked to fuck in the dark, but some light shone in through the blinds from the lamppost outside – the shadows fell on their bodies, stripes of human experience, savage yet delicately rhapsodic.

She turned over and he mounted her, covered her, and tried to put his cock in. Now, Marlene knew little about wolves or their anatomy – but she seemed to remember there was a penis hook involved that acted like nature's Velcro – locking the male and female together until the male's sperm had had a chance to impregnate his mate before any rival could try his luck. And Colin wasn't even here! In any case, the whole thing made her feel a little nervous. So, Robert had a

162

little trouble inserting himself, but putting his hand on the base of her back, he slowly managed it.

She gasped. She didn't like sex with humans never mind wolves – but novelty of it did something to her, she had to admit. And of course she knew it wasn't *a real fucking wolf, don't be fucking stupid – but then what the fuck was real anyway*? She had no idea anymore.

Robert took her roughly. Of course he did. The company of wolves, so it goes.

Animals never seem to enjoy sex. Marlene thought. She'd only seen pigeons shagging, and dogs of course, but she had the impression that the female just wanted it to finish as soon as it started – which, on an everyday basis, was just like her. So, yes, she agreed with herself, in that respect *you could call me an animal. You hear that dad, Branco, all you other fuckers and fuckwits – you've been calling me that for years and I agree, I'm a fucking animal.* She sang to herself: *She was a no-one who killed her baby/She sent her letters from the country/She was an animal/She was a bloody disgrace – and don't give me those looks,* she said to the dead

163

babies. The dead babies were staring at her. The dead babies were watching. Which, since one of the dead babies belonged to Robert, made this… a Primal Scene.

Pigs. She'd also seen pigs having a go at each other once. Quite a production. But she didn't like to think of pigs. She saw herself as quite pig like. And it wasn't a nice feeling. Pigs are quite ugly. *Ugly*. She almost dried up at the thought of it. *Ug face. Frog face.* Branco had left her for a girl with classic good looks. *I will castrate him, and will gut her. Frog face. That's what they used to call me.* But her dad said she was beautiful… inside. *I've got a face that will get better with age – I will grow into it. It will look better when I'm older.* She thought.

The world will love me. The fucking world – I will spit in its fucking eye. The world huffed and it puffed and tried to blow me the fuck down.

She squealed out loud. Robert thought it just the acid squealing. He didn't let it put him off his stroke. It was hard to distract him once he'd got going.

I'm a pig with a frog's face, groaned Marlene. Sometimes Robert liked to fuck in front of the mirror – *but there's no way I'm looking in any fucking mirrors on acid*, thought Marlene. Imagine! *But I'm beautiful person inside. My dad told me. The fucking great liar. Aren't you, dad? You cunt with your fucking cancer. He. Them. Boys. They tried to blow me down, and yes I blew some of them. But not my dad! They tried to tear me down. They tried to tear me. The big fucking bad wolf.*

She was glad that Robert was taking her from behind – she didn't want to look in his eyes. She didn't want to see a reflection of herself in his eyes. And she didn't want to share the wild feelings that had doubtless set his eyes alight.

'Do you want me to eat you?' whispered Robert in Marlene's ear.

'Nooo!' cried Marlene…

'OK, I was just asking,' said Robert, a little confused. Marlene never usually turned down the offer of oral sex.

165

Marlene looked back over her shoulder at him. She looked at his mouth. *Never realised how big it was. Wide. Sensuous. Enticing smile. But those teeth! My God how sharp they look.*

Marlene went into an acid reverie. A gothic fever dream.

'What a big mouth you have,' she said in a trembling voice to the wolf.

'All the better to eat you with!' growled the wolf, dressed in her mum's clothes, *no not my mum's*! – anyway, it was a strange looking wolf, it had a tail like a fox's and ears pricked like a dog's. *Probably symbolic*, she thought, now I'm really in trouble.

The wolf jumped out of bed, and ate her up in one lick, swallowing her whole. Then the beast, with a stomach full, sated, fell asleep, snoring – l*ike all these fuckers do after they've had what they wanted*, she thought. Marlene curled up in a foetal ball in the wolf's stomach, closed her eyes and dreamt. A dream within a dream.

A hunter who, weirdly, looked like a wolf himself, had appeared from the dark forest. He saw the wolf with the fat bulging stomach, as if pregnant.

'The wolf! He won't get away this time!' said the hunter.

And without further ado, he cut open the wolf's stomach. 'You'll never bother anyone ever again,' he said, shaking a fist that looked like a paw.

And to his utter amazement, from the wolf's stomach out popped Branco, Marlene's dad, Robert, a few dead kids, and some other horrible people, all saying really *ugly* things. Last but not least came Marlene herself.

She had been saved.

'Next time, keep to the path,' said the hunter who took Marlene – her hand in his paw and led her away...

'No!' cried Marlene in panic.

'OK, fine, I heard you, I won't go down on you!' said Robert, 'I wasn't suggesting anal sex or anything. Christ!'

The wolf and the ass – there is a fable in there somewhere, a ludicrous fairy tale. One with a moral.

'Do you know the Aesop fable?' he asked her. 'The wolf and the ass.'

Marlene didn't. But pondered. Perhaps Robert wasn't the wolf, perhaps he was the ass in wolf's clothing?

Just as she was beginning to come around to the idea that maybe Robert only looked like a wolf, he bent down and bit her on the spot where neck and shoulder meet. Hard.

While Robert had been steadily fucking Marlene, he had increasingly come to realise that something was wrong. He fucked her this way. He fucked her that way. He stroked her breasts. He sniffed her belly button. He sniffed her arse. She just didn't feel or smell like herself – sour and bitter. Now she smelt: mass-produced. With a chemical tang that scrambled Robert's senses a little more, if that was possible. And she felt to the touch: fabricated. He stroked her hair – how stiff it was. Like a wig. Her pubes, too. They were obviously man made. That was it. Marlene was made of plastic! But was she some kind of life-sized plastic model? Or, was she a blow up doll? He suspected the latter – the innermost her behind the veil.

He hated the thought that he was fucking a blow up doll. He once knew a guy who knew a guy who worked in a Soho sex shop. The guy sold a doll to a Chinese chap. Later that day, the man came back to return the doll – deflated, stuffed crudely back in the box, obviously used. What was wrong with it? 'Ah so!' said the man. The Soho guy said: 'Sorry?' The man pointed to the crotch. 'No, ah so.' 'Ah so?' 'Yes, ah so!' 'Oh.' It clicked, the plastic sex doll was not equipped with an anus. Crushed, the backdoor man had brought it back. Robert laughed when he heard the story – but understood where the guy was coming from – or not as the case may be.

Still the idea of fucking a blow up doll didn't amuse him – he didn't want to be like the Soho tossers. He was better than that. There was only one way to find out the truth about this doll business… he bent down as if to kiss Marlene, bared his teeth and bit.

'Argh,' shouted Marlene, muting herself quickly after remembering their neighbours. 'What the fuck do you think you're doing?' she stage whispered.

Well, she didn't burst or quickly deflate, but Robert still wasn't completely sure whether or not she was a blow up doll. Every picture of a blow-up doll he'd seen had been as ugly as sin, with an asymmetric body. The Soho sex shop guy had remarked, 'Never mind about the lack of arse, who would want to fuck someone who looks like a frog princess with Downs Syndrome?' Not a nice thing to say. Robert resolved not to repeat that to Marlene. He asked her straight: 'Look, are you a blow up doll or not, Marlene?'

'What?' She exclaimed. 'I'll fucking blow you up. You stupid cunt.' She wanted to lash out but restrained herself.

Robert turned Marlene onto her back, raised her legs over his shoulders and, realising his time in Marlene was perhaps approaching an end, took her hard and fast.

He looked at her naked left foot by his face. Robert didn't really like Marlene's feet – they were too claw-like, lacking sensuality. But sometimes a naked foot is a naked foot – and that is enough. He started to come.

He looked down and saw that his penis was no longer engorged flesh, pulsing with sperm, but a fountain – a large ornate fountain in a sunny city – one that gushed water from its spout – a steady surge that continued for hours, days, aeons – like time lapse filming – with those sped-up clouds flying across the screen – and finally, after eternity, after generations had been born, had lived, gone about their lives as best they could, and died – finally, the water from the baroque fountain stopped. The world was left to lament that the beautiful fountain had dried up. The fountain fed by, and feeding all of the rivers, lakes, seas and oceans in the world had emptied itself, and the world felt regret.

Robert pulled his cock out, a last drop of liquid fell on Marlene's pubes. He flopped on the bed exhausted. Marlene dug him in the ribs with her fist.

'Oof,' he said.

'Ah so,' said Marlene.

'What?'

'Arsehole. Have you ever seen your own arsehole?' she asked him.

This was obviously a philosophical riddle, one that Robert would ponder over for years to come.

15.

get the picture?

One day, Marlene came back from somewhere, and flopped down on the bed. She didn't say where she'd been, but Robert presumed she'd been with Colin, taking drugs and having some sort of sex.

Robert thought the scene before him, Marlene face down on the bed, silver/white cropped hair, the light pouring in and out via the window above the bed, skirt pulled down slightly at the back, half exposing large silver/white buttocks, bare feet, looked like a tainted pop statement, either a warm up or aftermath to a porn shoot, a murder scene, an anti-glamour crisis, or a sensitive meditation on form and (what's the) matter. All of that.

He snapped the scene two or three times on his Kodak instant. The pictures developed in front of his very eyes. Magic.

In the future, Robert mused on whether or not one of these photos would work as a cover for a book – the one describing this story.

His friend Boogie said the pictures were too much like Nan Goldin's.

Robert loved Goldin. He'd recently seen her *Memory Lost* exhibition in London. He wrote about it for an arts journal.

'Although *Memory Lost*, the centre piece of *Sirens*, Nan Goldin's first solo exhibition for 12 years looks backwards, comprising old work both previously seen and unseen, it's far from being a simple retrospective – and it's clear why Goldin herself considers it to be a major fresh work.

'*Memory Lost* is a 45-minute slideshow of pictures, music and dialogue, the main theme of which is addiction.

'The slideshow format – *a la* her ground breaking work *The Ballad of Sexual Dependency* – is perfect for

174

Goldin's oeuvre. Images pulse and disappear: a flickering zoetrope of pictures – almost ephemeral – like a drug rush, a hit; easy come easy go easy come again.

'We see:-

'… Cookie Mueller, smouldering with a certain confused impatience… drugs… Religious icons (kitsch – the chosen iconography style of melodrama and excess), milk/water flowing from a statuette's breasts…

'It's also a fast flow of feelings; as if to maintain that it isn't actually true that life isn't worth living unless you pause now and then to reflect that you are alive.

'… a drooping, withered Xmas tree … messy hotel rooms… wrecked rooms… disturbing self-portraits (a molten/bemused quality in her eyes, as though she had seen or imagined bad sad things – especially in the mirror, perhaps)…

'The show is carried by the type of rhythm that opens up the borders of slippery psychological complexity.

175

'... New York City... the projects... a horrific slit wrist... drugs... a drug neighbourhood... a shitty mattress ruined by a large 'fall-unconscious-with-a-cigarette' hole burnt all the way through, springs and wires exposed like nerves...

'Art and fame, sex and money all blurred together like wild forces we can't control.

'... pills in an open safe ...

'It's a revelation, almost traumatic – art that feels like a physical sensation. Emotions drift like the swirls in a drug user's spoon.

'The visuals are underpinned by a haunting, doleful new score by composer Mica Levi, which takes the dread to the next level. The dialogue, comprising phone messages and snippets of conversations, overlays the music and the pictures with musings and utterances benumbed – from or about people who, at some point, have lost the thread of the track of their own lives:-

'... coke or dope... wake up...wake up...wake up... wake up... in mom's arms, that's where I felt safe and secure... I would put 'dead' by people's names but then there were so many I gave up... are you OK? Call me. Are you eating? What's happening? ... I couldn't leave the house – the beautiful leaves turning making me ... it must be the fall ... the fall... just trying not to feel anything... you don't ever belong... took the money and keys and left me in the room for five days – I couldn't get drugs and it was like being buried alive... he doesn't know how to cry anymore – just makes noises... connection – that's what people are looking for in addiction...

'Goldin came to prominence by presenting, with bravery, empathy and downbeat pizzazz, the 'holy moment' of photography, when the camera's gaze alights on the real, however provocative it may be: fixed, unspeakable reality. Fixed and unspeakable perhaps because, as writer Ann Marlowe says, addiction – and it was always there in the background – stops time – physically, emotionally, philosophically – it is "a form of mourning for irrecoverable glories". In other words, nostalgia in its most alarming form – one which "stops your passage to the future".

'In this respect, *Memory Lost* is anything but nostalgic. Instead – and this is the point – it reframes, recasts, recalibrates the past in order to present an arc. That of the subjects who embody *Memory Lost*'s theme – it recognises that head, heart and psyche of the drug user is either filled with light or horror, depending on the point travelled on the spiral. And that of the artist herself – asserting that memory is not a fixed concept and that we can and do recontextualize to make sense of a given narrative – and it's this that offers nothing less and nothing more than a sense of fresh possibility.'

Robert thought: I know this life, I know this art, I am glad that Goldin has found redemption.

He decided not to put one of the Kodak instant photos on the cover of the book.

16.

a compelling tale

Some hours later. The sun had come up, spreading warmth. Robert and Marlene were on the bed, freezing. But still naked. The acid had worn off to a large degree. They had both had enough.

Robert was no longer able to look into the future at will. The visions of unfolding events that he had seen and felt, would not be remembered. Sometimes, over the years, he would get the feeling that something very valuable had been in his embrace, his possession. But he could not remember exactly what. It was like a dream that he would forever try to recall. Also, he knew, even though it was a platitude – *people forever veer from platitudes to dramatics and back*, he thought – that the only way to tell the future was to make it. Truly make it.

The voices in Marlene's head had stopped for the time being.

Robert could see the defining black lines of the colouring book very clearly once more.

'Bloop!' he said very softly as an understated finale, for old time's sake.

But the wild hallucinations had been replaced by the sense that they were both looking at the world through a slightly dirty Perspex screen. There was a barrier between themselves and what they saw. It was almost ironic – the revenge of the Gods – that they, who had always held the normal world in contempt, were now removed from it – they both wrung their hands in consternation and agony. One definition of hell is simply separation from God, so Robert and Marlene's Hell was separation from the normal world. They could not touch it, or feel it – it was as though they had both been put in a small cell from which they could vaguely view the outside, but not take part in it on any level. Two damned souls writhing. They desperately wanted nothing more than for everything to be as it always had been. Instead, their feelings had been bleached out, and it had been this way for a while. Robert, who was interested in the idea of 'distance', 'remoteness' and cool, was now trapped tightly in a vast cold space.

For how long, he wondered?

Marlene started to cry. She would have sobbed her heart out, *if she had one*, joked Robert to himself.

'It's going to be like this forever, isn't it?' she said, panicking. 'We're like those casualties you hear about – the ones who've gone out too far and can never come back.'

Robert said nothing. And he didn't hold Marlene to comfort her.

'Next time, let's just take speed,' she said. 'If there is a next time. If I'm not in a loony bin. I can't take this anymore. I want to come back.'

Robert took his mind off the situation by working out how this part of story could be written up, or filmed, maybe. He envisaged a loop of the scene broken down into different parts – but the dialogue accompanying each part would change at random – so it would never ever be the same. Out of sync, too, Robert added as an afterthought. Perfect dislocation.

'We just have to let the acid wear off completely, don't worry,' he said. But he was a little concerned himself – he'd never know the tail end of a trip, with its very real sense of dissociation to last for so long. Perhaps they *would* be eternal drug victims. But, no, that would be crazy, it would be punishment outweighing the crime – an injustice – and he was a person who believed in natural justice. Justice just is, as it were.

He said: 'We just have to wait.'

Marlene continued to cry.

He repeated: 'Just wait.'

And so they waited. Naked and afraid.

Marlene waited: -

... to say to herself: I have been dispossessed of my identity, *I* have dispossessed myself of my identity.

... for all the pity in this world and the next.

... to recognise the qualities and benefits of anxiety.

... for someone who would reveal herself to herself.

... for the ghost of her father to tell a joke. A good one.

... for the age of confession and spurious grievance.

... to paint a stupid and disturbing self-portrait.

... to stop the future and the past *and fucking let me off.*

... for anything but nostalgia.

... to make the mistake of putting knowledge above imagination.

... to assume the eternal values of the supermarket.

Robert waited:-

... to get paid for daydreaming.

... to richly possess a number of 'poor objects.'

... for a sign directing him to the last remote Badlands.

... to sit quietly in a room.

... to go uptown and downtown.

... for writing – his own, that is – which feels like a physical sensation.

... to realise that words are never enough.

... for 'soul food and a place to eat'.

They both waited:-

... For the taste of decay/death in their mouths to diminish. (Robert: *Corpse in my mouth? I'm a fucking vegan!*)

... to understand the real meaning of the phrase: the politics of boredom.

... to laugh *with* not *at* Kafka: 'There is hope – but not for *us*.'

... Zen silence.

... to become familiar characters to themselves.

... to disappear here, and there.

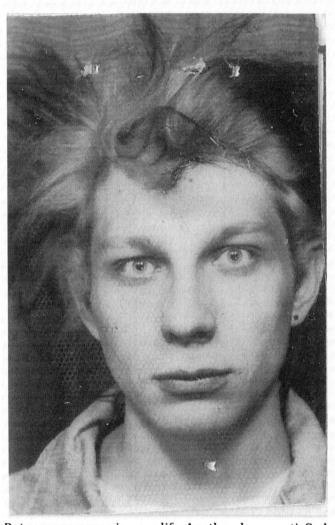

Put some romance in your life. Another dream satisfied.

POSTSCRIPT

Diary entries 1988-9

Tuesday April 19 1988

Reviewing Frank Zappa at the Wembley Arena. Meet
Terry. Drinks in Soho, drinks in Wembley, drinks at the
party afterwards, drinks at Terry's till 6am: I slid into
oblivion to wake up in a Hackney hell hole, fully clothed
with a duvet thrown over me. XXXX and XXXX arrive
with three dogs – one of them very licky. I resign
myself to wasting another day through alcohol. Not
only waste but suffer – my come downs are enormous;
depression – I feel like weeping uncontrollably, mainly
cause I have to work and all I want to do is curl up with
a book. But I must be Jeffrey Bernard about it – a guy
who was sacked many times for drunkenness beyond
the call of duty.

Wednesday April 27 1988

... illness seeping through me but I don't realise it till I
awake after a night of being physically crushed and

187

hung upside down in a little ball and twisted around by a huge pair of hands like a malleable piece of green snot... experiences and joy = progress of soul but ditto the shit of nothing in private and personal hell of sterility – where is the fame and respect owed to a serious artist of the wastelands who isn't a real artist?

Thursday April 23 1988

I am a disgrace to the human race...

Wednesday May 4 1988

In West End, meet a crazed XXXX in tune with debauch and insanity. Drunk, she says she fucked XXXX, 'he was good' – I don't care. But she might regret it. Off to Camberwell where I fuck her on all fours. I put a finger up her ass, a shiny tube. She wiped the spunk from between her legs with my clean Seditionaries T shirt. Apt. I should get a wardrobe or rack – all those clothes I hang in the windows and around the room are fucked by the sun... then I went up to XXXX's to watch a bit of the *'66-'68* series on TV – Situationists and Co twenty years on – all the rebels are fatter and balder – just like the punks now – with nothing gained but regression, perhaps. Two ex-lovers talk about their time together, their betrayals. They seem empty and resigned to emptiness. *C'est la vie.* Not for me. We'll see. Keep going and hope for a break – yeah, break my heart.

Friday May 20 1988

Hung around some of the seedier Soho dives – including the Dive Bar, where I chatted to a cute girl – she didn't like Ray, who seemed to frighten the girls – he's socially inept, intense and shy, but come on, he's not frightening – before being dragged off to the Intrepid Fox, where I got distracted by blonde from Birmingham – kissed and then… later made my excuses and went up to XXXX's to watch *Letters from a Dead Man* – a Russian treatment of a post-nuclear holocaust situation. Romantic and philosophical. Poetic certainly. The West could never come up with something like this. I'm almost proud to originate in blood from this vague part of the world… I read the *NME* and discover they've printed hate letters directed towards me from Zappa fans about my review. Can't even remember

writing it... listen to a pirate reggae show on the radio –
it keeps me going.

Wednesday May 25 1988

XXXX rang me to say she missed me (!?), I was
supposed to meet her but... the Patrick Walker
horoscope warns me that the relationship set up will
have to be examined. I know... money is a worry.

Thursday June 2 1988

These days everyone sees life as a big mind game and a
battle. Everyone getting one up on everyone else. I
heard someone say: 'The good thing about being out of
it and being in an argument is the thought: if I were
straight I'd slaughter this guy.' What a wanker. The
nasty side has really come out in people nowadays.
People act like little kids all the time everywhere. If you
take people and society seriously – that's the way to
lose track and hope... bad phone call from XXXX –
picking at each other and I slammed the phone down...
this part of the journal was actually written sitting at

my desk instead of lying on the bed – an attempt to become a real writer. Real writers sit at desks.

Thursday June 23 1988

Missed out on reviewing the Big Audio Dynamite LP, had enough of the *NME*. It's rubbish and people like XXXX are part of the forces of conservatism, really. Should have gone to see Strummer at the Fridge, but it would have been yet another drunken whirl. I'm not in the mood. Although the prospect of seeing XXXX is enticing. To fuck her little arse and make her squeal – like Saturday, sucking her cunt avidly, which may have produced moans, I don't know. I put it in her. She came two or three times – it always amazes me when I make someone come. To end off the romance I called her a beautiful girl and she called me a beautiful boy. Then I had a piss.

Monday June 27 1988

A disturbing dream. I and a group of people/friends are in the garden of a house – Dunstable? – a tower dominates the immediate skyline. As if it were on top of

191

the Dunstable Downs and the Downs were my garden. The tower leans, begins to fall. Tottering on the edge. Dilapidated. It's inevitable. In slow motion almost. We run back into the house. In apparent security we listen to chunks of it falling all around. I remember no more – I am under the tower that falls!

Wednesday July 6 1988

The 'squat' / housing association place in Camberwell may be a run-down tip, but at least I have the mental free space to forge some sort of future for myself… meet XXXX to talk convulsively about desperation (mine), future (hers) and Gorbachov – the beer spins in us and we fall in bed – I can't even remember how we fucked except just shoving it into her and then wetting XXXX's fingers with my spit and placing them on her clit until she whimpered for mercy so I stopped and fell asleep. This was the beginning of my downfall – my thoughts next day were scattered and work left unfinished – time is running out and I'm running after it.

Tuesday July 12 1988

Do I have a destiny or am I a slug? Am I a man or a slug slithering into oblivious obscurity leaving a shiny/dull trail that people, if they notice it, probably won't even wonder what happened to the slug that made it. I'm in a limp-cock backwater, which I'm treading, head just above the surface.

Tuesday July 12 1988

Rehearsals with new band, Woman – creativity introduced into the order of the day – I extend myself on guitar – I wanked my broken down shit Shaftesbury guitar – but I probably need a Strat... Meet Jane Suck at the *NME*. She tells me to fuck off. I tell her to fuck off. We fuck off.

Sunday July 30 1988

Recover from XXXX from King Kurt's party. Talked at length to thin, old Kings Road shop manager (Smiths) – making cracks, getting slapped. Then she invited me to the Grove tomorrow (today). I'm not sure. I can't get drunk again. It just leads to vegetation. My 80s: Half vegetable half animal.

Friday August 5 1988

Up very late and feel sick with myself for drinking. Dejected. Saved from myself by Jack who drags me off to guitar playing and… drinks. We chat over the usual emotions. Can't get inside this diary, or my own head. 'Love is a ghost'. Overwhelming sense of defeat, futility. XXXX's phone is dead which is lucky because I would have taken her out for a drink – and I would have felt bored and bad.

Monday August 8 1988

So the newspapers have pointed out, today is the eighth month of the eighty eighth (and a hundred) year. 8.8.88. In China they're going mental – the inauguration of their biggest building has been left till now, the maternity wards have been booked etc. In England no one gives a shit. It's not a case of superstition, but one of care about the universe and one's position in it. The bottom line being, if you make a date important it will become important. And how have I spent this magical day? Wondering how to transform my existence, that is how. Deciding not to feel guilty about the past, to realise that my present position means fuck all, and that I need to (make a) move.

Saturday August 13 1988

In the sun up at Brockwell Park, but the lido wasn't open. At night, the Loughborough Junction hotel. XXXX chatted to me while I sat on the bar over her – she brushed my knees and smiled up. We fucked for three hours. I tied her legs and made her hold her arms above her head. Talked incessant obscenities into her ears. I spurted into her. She wanted me to suck her off. 'You expect me to put my tongue down there after I've just come?' I said. 'Just keep it above, on my clit,' she said. And I did... next day sun and sea in Sussex. Later Sussex in the dark – tree shapes with, surely, their spirits freaking about at the roadside. Revelling in the dusk. Weary travellers saved only by the roadside coffee inns. Preferable, the echoes of ritual and unbridled nature – wandering of villagers, mob, tribe and highwayman, to the violent modern suburbia...

195

Education: Me: 'When will the world wake up to my talent?' XXXX: 'When will you wake up?'

Sunday August 25 1988

… my orgasm was impeded by an unrolled foreskin! I just stared into space…

Monday September 5 1988

I feel negative and depressed. Patrick Walker in the *Standard* says 'be more optimistic'. What does he know. It comes down to my desires and needs. Maybe I need security? Heavenly, bestial cuties are for youngsters, who cares about that when you get older? Maybe a woman with her own place and a yearning for kids and some unhurried weekends should be what I'm aiming for? In any event, it is time to move on. Where? To the wasteland? I am already here… XXXX comes round and we drink four pints in the Canning. She's a wild child. And she worries me. XXXX phones later. Pete Clag is dead. Died in his sleep from 'natural causes'. If being an alcoholic is natural that is. I looked out of the window and spooked myself out. Mortality touched us all that night. I won't make the funeral. I will write a letter of condolence to KW, whose review I did not write. Still, you can't please everyone.

Thursday October 20 1988

Interviewed XXXX XXXX in his flat. I ask if he ever gets lonely. He says, 'I suppose so. Everyone does. If you haven't got kids your life has to be your work. What else is there, just get pissed all the time?' Yeah, there has to be something more. I am becoming boring.

Monday October 31 1988

Halloween. The Union of Christian Teachers are applying pressure to have this pagan and evil festival banned. I don't care. I'm doing nothing to celebrate it. Selfish of me. This is a time to remember the dead and I should think of Daniela, and I do. But I feel something in the atmosphere. Apprehension, melancholy, fear. Or is it because I've spent three days curled up with XXXX (why was I going to say Daniela then?) and now I'm out on my own in the big wide world. On my own. People are out having fun. Some of us have to stay in and worry about the future.

Saturday November 6 1988

Met Terry in the Cambridge. I drank blackcurrant juice – ah the joys of being teetotal for a night. He's off to Portugal. Split with XXXX again. Living like a tramp I just realised, but his vision is magical – ' From the walls/wars of Persia to the French Revolution there is an unbroken chain. A big wall around us. Leading to America, designed to get us to Sirius. The Russians fit in as being Mongolian. The Wicca people want to retain the earth.' I like it. He's mad, of course.

Monday November 14 1988

Why am I writing so strangely? So rhetorically? Loosen up! My speech has assumed a clipped, meaningful tone, but where has the zest and colour gone? … rash on my arms. Vaguely worrying… XXXX's floundering about, looking for a future, just like everyone else. She has a panic stricken crying fit. Then we share a freaky

boredom which we don't explore. But we hold hands...
none of it is enough.

Sunday November 27 1988

Bile in my system. Wanted to be alone. Claustrophobia.
But went to see old Anarchist films – the Situationists,
cadre against cadre – hopeless. Cold Hackney. Cold.

Tuesday January 3 1989

Tarot for the New Year.

Situation – Queen of Wands/ Seven of Wands/Four of
Wands
Future One – Ace of Cups/FOOL/Eight of Pentacles
Future Two – Three of Wands/EMPEROR/STAR
Psychological basis – Two of Pentacles/Knight of
Pentacles/Four of Pentacles
Karma – FORTUNE/DEATH/10 of Swords

Situation – Energy at last gasp, obstacles but must get
courage to meet them, persistent energy needed.
Future One – Fertility, ideas, new era, new error

199

Future Two – Success after struggle, power, hope and clarity.

Psychological basis – harmony and dullness

Karma – Change of fortune, sudden and unexpected change, disruption.

Wednesday January 25 1989

But, God (why am I talking to God? Why not?), I should be exploring ways of beating reality and not just escaping it. I'm just avoiding it for the time being. I'm interviewing the Shamen. Jeez, what do I care about these people? Nothing… XXXX is always ill. Maybe I should get her something for the weekend – like a doctor. Let's pray she hasn't got AIDS, or I've got it, too. How selfish? Bought a mountain bike, £125 plus £16.50p lock – I will save £34 in Capital Cards for the next month.

Monday 13 February 1989

Rolled around Soho with Terry and then did it all over again next night at the Johnny Thunders gig. Terry had a drug dealer smashing up his room and fucking his ex.

Who needs it? How come my journal is just full of moans and hopes and not the in-depth look at art and humanity that it should be?

Friday February 17 1989

Lonely. But then at the Grove. Met XXXX – God knows why I ever had a thing with her. Her mate XXXX is a real human and a laugh. Told her she'd look great with a pair of knuckledusters on. Good chat up line!

Monday February 20 1989

Reading *Wonderland Avenue* by Danny Sugerman for the interview – heroin and cocaine, the Whiskey, Rainbow Rooms, Sunset Boulevard, collapse, hospital, psychiatrist. The moral of the story: be rich or have a rich father. But the real moral of the story: stop fucking about and get down to write and write. XXXX gone to LA (to meet Danny Sugerman?) I've got to find something. I need something.

Sunday March 5 1989

I'm short of breath and short of friends. Fucked XXXX in the morning, and she put a Johnny on me – but the phone rang , and it rang for ages and ages and it put me off. I couldn't help thinking it was bad news, Or good. It gets to be the same thing in a way. And then I thought of maybe get some speed, maybe pay my tax, about how I hate that guy who works for the *Record Mirror* on my production journalism course, and about the girl on the course whose mum works for that Catholic paper and wonder if I'd like to fuck her, and about flavoured Johnnies and about how expensive driving lessons are and I better pass my test soon and... I couldn't really come and wondered whether I should fake it. Why not?

Tuesday March 28 1989

I'm worried that all my friends have left or are leaving. But I'm here to stay. Worried that what I'm saying is just an exercise in writing and not from the heart. It is. But I can't hear myself. My voice. I am worried then that I am not a writer... drunk with XXXX at the Sonic Youth gig, first at the Warwick Arms down the

Portobello Road – XXXX XXXX called my ex, Marlene, a dyke. Yeah. But I still had a go at him. I got beer all over myself somehow.

Saturday March 1 1989

Latin night at the Alexandra, Clapham. Danced with XXXX who asked about XXXX, but still kissed me. Ah who cares? Patrick Walker says 13 aspects (whatever they are) are hurtling into my sign. Can I handle it? Ooh...

Wednesday April 19 1989

I just want to sleep in sweet oblivion. I need to be more cheerful – like Tom Jones, he had no friends, no money but a smile *and* a whistle on his lips. And he was pretty. Tom Jones.

Diary ends.

APPENDIX

Select Bibliography

The following books were important/essential to me (and to the characters) during the period covered in *Looking for a Kiss* – 1984-89. The selection is confined to those books which I still own – i.e. those which I had access to while writing (books are for touching/feeling). I've listed them in the same order as they are arranged on my shelves.

Jean Genet – *Our Lady of the Flowers*

Friedrich Nietzsche – *Ecce Homo: How One Becomes What One Is*
(The chapter titles rock: 'Why I Am So Wise', 'Why I Am So Clever' 'Why I Write Such Good Books' and 'Why I Am a Destiny' etc)

Kenneth Grant – *Aleister Crowley and the Hidden God*

Albert Camus – *The Fall*

Dave Wallis – *Only Lovers Left Alive*

Robert Anton Wilson – *Illuminatus* trilogy (The most interesting thing about SF, some would say, is its dystopian drift. The genre twitches if not bulges with works containing a pulse-pounding progressive inclination complete with overarching themes that speak of anxieties about and enthusiasms for the unravelling of society. Eschewing pseudo rationality and techno fetishism such works deal not so much with prediction, but instead hold a mirror up to the present. Radical ideas are applied to fantastic narratives by writers like Orwell, Dick, and Dave Wallis (*Only Lovers Left Alive*). But the grooviest, hottest and horniest of these is surely Robert Anton Wilson, high and fly and way too wet to dry. I met Wilson in the early 80s, when he was living in Dublin. He told me the city suited him because the four faces of the town hall clock each presented a different time. People called it the Four Liars. This chimed with Bob's sense of humour and philosophical outlook. 'I do not believe in anything but I have my suspicions,' he once said. Wilson's most rigorous attack on the dogmatism of 'reality' – one of his mottos was 'Beware of the Dogma' – came via the 800-page epic the *Illuminatus* trilogy (1975). This is a potted history of the world and a searing assault on the tricksy savagery of politicians and politics. The sprawling structure is underpinned by anything that can be used for fun and kicks – drugs, the occult, sex, and conspiracy theory. It's a riot of dissonance and discord. Very funny with it, though. One reviewer called it 'a fairy story for paranoiacs.' But fairy tales can teach us what text books can't – about the power of mystery and about how reason and logic are not the be all. In *Illuminatus* Wilson slugs it out in the artistic and philosophical arena, drawing on Burroughs, Joyce, Crowley, Ginsberg, Bakunin *et al* in the tussle between convention and progress, the citizen and the state, the Man and men. Not to mention the hepcats and the deadbeats, the solid senders and the squares and the Righteous and the rotten. It's an eternal fight. In the late 70s and early 80s I most encountered *Illuminatus* in the punk squats, crash pads and art labs around London town, in the hands of those on the margins looking for some action and magic.)

Anne Kavan – *Ice* ('What I saw had no solidity, it was all made of mist and nylon, with nothing behind.')

Antonin Artaud – *Artaud Anthology* (Given to me in the 70s by my late cousin, Peter, who, I thought, had a touch of the Artaud about him, and he thought the same about me – that was a little worrying, but I guess we all go through our Antonin A period, no?)

Samuel Beckett – *Molloy*

Susan Sontag – *On Photography*

Virginia Woolf – *To the Lighthouse*

Patti Smith – *Ha! Ha! Houdini!*, *Witt*, *The Night* (with Tom Verlaine) – (I bought all of these one afternoon in the summer of 1976 from Compendium Books in Camden. I had spent the morning at the Oval watching the West Indies thrash England. I wasn't a cricket fan, so I'm not sure what I was doing there. But I remember the atmosphere was great – more like a raucous football match. The Patti Smith books were pretty cool, too. On the same visit I also bought one or two issues of the great reggae fanzine *Pressure Drop*.)

Henry Miller – *Sexus, Plexus, Nexus*

Colin Wilson – *The Occult* (everyone's 1970s entrée into mysticism. Mine included. Wilson's value lay in his ability to write clearly, concisely yet passionately about subjects that seldom received such treatment. Without resorting to boring 'easy way to learn' methods he put topics like the sexual impulse, mysticism and psychology at the layman's fingertips. Wilson was a pop writer. Pop was cool. Pop is cool.)

Brett Easton Ellis – *Less Than Zero*, *Rules of Attraction* ('"Nothing. Nothing makes me happy. I like nothing," I tell her.')

Danny Sugerman – *Wonderland Avenue: Tales of Glamour and Excess* (' "Life in the fast lane"… "What a fucking joke. Everyone knows there are no lanes in a demolition derby."')

William Hughes – *Performance* (The book of the film, which made for astonishing viewing at Scala cinema all-nighters – a place renown for action off screen as well as on).

Eve Babitz – *Slow Days, Fast Company* ('No one burned hotter than Eve Babitz. Possessing skin that radiated "its own kind of moral laws,"')

Cookie Mueller – *Walking Through Clear Water*

Kathy Acker – *Blood and Guts in High School* (I wasn't sure about KA – but I liked her rawness and honesty. She never seemed to be out simply to shock; her subject matter was her natural vision. Her streets were gutters and the kids played at junky and whore instead of Cowboy and Indian, as they say.)

Knut Hamsun – *Hunger*

Emmett Grogan – *Ringolevio*

Aleister Crowley – *Confessions of Aleister Crowley*, *Moonchild*, *Diary of a Drug Fiend*, *Book of Thoth*

Fred and Judy Vermorel – *Sex Pistols: The Inside Story*, *Starlust* (I liked Fred, but we had our misunderstandings at one time. I was going to, with Jane Suck, co-write a front cover *Time Out* piece on

Fred until he learned about my involvement and nixed it. But I eventually forgave him.)

Raymond Chandler – Everything.

Alexander Baron – *Lowlife*

Charles Bukowski – *Post Office, Ham on Rye, You Get so Alone at Times* ('I wasn't much of a petty thief. I wanted the whole world or nothing.')

Joe Orton – *The Orton Diaries*

Greil Marcus – *Lipstick Traces* (Great launch, or what I can remember of it!)

William Burroughs Jnr – *Speed*

Jim Carroll – *Basketball Diaries*

Martin Millar – *Milk, Sulphate and Alby Starvation*

Guy Debord – *The Society of the Spectacle*

Mervyn Peake – *Gormenghast* trilogy

Andy Warhol – *Popism*, *The Philosophy of*, *Diaries of*

Barry Miles – *Ginsberg*

William Gibson – *Burning Chrome*, *Neuromancer*

JG Ballard – *Concrete Island*

Diane di Prima – *Memoirs of a Beatnik*

Hermine Demoriane – *The Tightrope Walker* (She popped around to my flat once, unannounced. I had no idea how she'd got my address. People used to do that sort of thing in the 80s. We had tea and talked about Derek Jarman, Jean Luc-Godard (she'd interviewed him) and punk. Tightrope walking didn't come up.)

Milton – *Paradise Lost*

Raymond Carver – *What We Talk About When We Talk About Love*

Mick Farren – *Watch Out Kids*

Jay McInerney – *Bright Lights, Big City*

Colin McCabe – *Godard: Images, Sounds, Politics*

Jan Cremer – *I, Jan Cremer* (For a while I played in a band called Woman (with one of the original members of King Kurt, amongst others). Our best song was *I'm Here to Stay*, a paean to the wild Beatnik artist Cremer)

James Joyce – *Ulysses* (I studied English Literature at the Polytechnic of North London, radical hotbed of revolt in the 70s. I took little away from this experience, apart from a poor degree and, far more importantly, a love and appreciation of this book.)

Jean Stein – *Edie*

John Berger – *Ways of Seeing*

Roland Barthes – *Mythologies*

William Burroughs – *Junky*

Richard Neville – *Playpower*

Jim Dodge – *Not Fade Away*

Jeffrey Bernard – *Low Life* (The only reason to read *The Spectator*, *The Sunday Mirror* or thinking-man's-freebie *Midweek* in the 80s was for the Soho drunk's Low Life column – 'a suicide note written in weekly instalments'. Tony D and I wasted so much time and cash in those same Soho pubs – Tony said: 'If I saved all the money that I spent on drink, I'd spend it on drink.' I think he nicked that off someone else. Probably Bernard.)

Jean Paul Sartre – *Roads to Freedom*

Richard Yates – *Revolutionary Road*

Nelson Algren – *Never Come Morning, Neon Wilderness*

Ed Sanders – *Tales of Beatnik Glory*

Peter York – *Style Wars*

GI Gurdjieff – *Meetings with Remarkable Men*

Andrew Arato – *Essential Frankfurt School Reader*

Ingmar Bergman – *Scenes from a Marriage*

George Bataille – *Blue of Noon* (Ostensibly *Blue Of Noon*
is Bataille's overtly political novel. His approach brings
to mind the more instinctive aspects of De Sade. Like
De Sade, Bataille wants 'everything' and 'all at once' –
which is to demand the 'impossible' (let's be
reasonable)– 'a permanent revolution of the spirit'.)

Victor Bockris – *The Life and Death of Andy Warhol*, *Up-
Tight: Velvet Underground Story*

Alexander Trocchi – *Young Adam*

Isabelle Collin Dufresne (Ultra Violet) – *Famous for 15
minutes*

Dorothy Parker – *The Portable Dorothy Parker*

John Wyndham – *Day of the Triffids*

John Christopher – *Death of Grass*

Paul Sieveking – *Man Bites Man: The Scrapbook of an Edwardian Eccentric* (I went around his house once, you know. Fascinating chap. Ex-editor of the *Fortean Times*, amongst other wonderful things – such as producing the first English translation of Raoul Vaneigem's *The Revolution of Everyday Life*)

Pauline Reage – *Story of O*

Gerald Kersh – *Night and the City*

Lenny Bruce – *The Essential Lenny Bruce* (We had something of a renaissance of hard 'alternative comedy' on our hands with 'crazies' like Sam Kinneson and Gerry Sadowitz. Their outrageous nature harkened all the way back to the Sick Comic himself, Lennie Bruce – also called the Sickest of the Sick ,The Crown Prince of Dope, The Man From Outer Taste. Reason enough to love him right there – another was his finding a single comprehensive metaphor for human experience. One that stripped away all the lies.)

Marquis de Sade – *Justine, Juliette*

Phillip K Dick – *Ubik*

Anthony Burgess – *Clockwork Orange*

Stephen Koch – Stargazer (I reviewed this one for the *NME*, and wrote something like: this pins Warhol down in the underground of the Duchampian *avant garde*. *Edie*, *Popism* etc may be the great anecdotal documentaries of the era, but *Stargazer* is a fine analysis of the madness which pulsed through the Factory like a heartbeat. The Factory, a spectacle created from various strands of themes that Warhol's films actually balance on. Withdrawal, passivity and inauthenticity. If Warhol could make his peace with all this, others could not – the casualty list was long. As Koch notes, though, Warhol's 'avenging demon' turned out to be not suicide but murder. In effect Valerie Solanas did not fail. The gaunt master of the passive spectacle was stopped short… Shortly afterwards, the *NME* junked its book reviews page – the downward curve had begun.)

Mark P – *The Bible*

Dennis Morris – *Rebel Rock* (Believe In The Ruins/The Only Notes That Matter Are The Ones That Come In Wads.)

Nat Finkelstein – *Andy Warhol*

Jamie Reid – *Up they Rise* (I asked Jamie to sign my copy: 'I owe it all to you, Richard' He didn't seem too pleased, but wrote it all the same.)

William Powell – *Anarchist Cookbook*

ACKNOWLEDGEMENTS AND CREDITS

Cover photograph and design – Millie Radaković

Author biography photograph – Millie Radaković

Photographs 1 and 3 – Joan Geoffroy, © Mick Mercer (pages 8 and 157)

Photographs 2 and 4 – Richard Cabut archive © Richard Cabut (pages 80 and 186)

Thank you: Zak and Laura at Sweat Drenched Press, Millie Radaković, Mick Mercer, Paul T Kirk, David Erdos, Ulrika Nappér and Johny Brown (NB one n only – Johny)

AUTHOR'S BIOGRAPHY

Richard Cabut is author of *Dark Entries* (Cold Lips Press, 2019), co-editor/-writer of the anthology *Punk is Dead: Modernity Killed Every Night* (Zer0 Books, October 2017), contributor to *Ripped, Torn and Cut – Pop, Politics and Punks Fanzines From 1976* (Manchester University Press, 2018) and *Growing Up With Punk* (Nice Time, 2018).

His journalism has featured in the *Guardian*, the *Daily Telegraph*, *NME* (pen name Richard North), *ZigZag*, *The Big Issue*, *Time Out*, *Offbeat* magazine, the *Independent*, *Artists & Illustrators* magazine, *thefirstpost*, London Arts Board/Arts Council England, *Siren* magazine, *International Times*, *Eyeplug*, etc

His short fiction has appeared in the books *The Edgier Waters* (Snowbooks, 2006) and *Affinity* (67 Press, 2015).

He was a Pushcart Prize nominee 2016.

Other literary pieces have featured in *Paris Bitter Hearts Spring* magazine, *Foggy Plasma* magazine, *Intellectual Refuge*, *3AMagazine*, *Zouch*, *Descent*.

Richard's plays have been performed at various theatres in London and nationwide, including the Arts Theatre, Covent Garden, London.

He published the fanzine *Kick*, and played bass for the punk band Brigandage (LP *Pretty Funny Thing* – Gung Ho Records, 1986).

richardcabut.com